Isla McNeese

War and Love in the West

By Philip Dampier

Summer 2022

Introduction

The Union Pacific section of the Transcontinental Railroad, under the guidance of Chief Engineer Grenville Dodge, brought the railroad tracks to Crow's Creek in southeast Wyoming on November 13, 1867. The tracks and then the trains brought settlers and workers in droves to the new city of Cheyenne, which grew up in the railroad's shadow in what was then the Idaho Territory. Soon a bustling, thriving and growing city flowed along the newly laid tracks.

Entrepreneurs were soon followed by cattlemen and their cows. Because cows drink a lot of water, arguments over water rights outside the city inevitably proved troublesome. The number of ranches grew as did the number of thirsty livestock. It was a tragedy in the making. Seemingly nothing could slow or halt the mixed population flowing into the Cheyenne area and then out into the surrounding valleys.

They came, freed black men, foreigners, disillusioned Civil War veterans, drifters, gamblers, and people looking for a fresh start or running from a bad past. The Wyoming Territory took them in, found room in rapidly growing towns along the railroad, or scattered them out on the prairies. The law was not as fast to come as the lawless. Some created their own law.

Part One: Late Summer

I heard the valley calling me,

Come, it said, come to my valley,

Smell the flowers emerging along the creek,

Feel the gentle wind sharing the sounds of birds,

Touch the waving blades of tall grass spreading
everywhere,

The sun is warm and good and you will prosper.

There are deer and antelope and bison to provide,

You will be happy in my valley.

ONE

Isla (*I-la*) McNeese sat straight in the saddle, her back warming to the early morning sun. Her horse, a tall chestnut, stood at the edge of the current, the water pushing by his hooves. Isla took in the land in front of her, a slight rise moving to the westward horizon covered with long-stemmed grasses dancing in the ever-blowing wind. The buds at the ends of the stems seem to be weaving and dodging the advances of dragonflies and the occasional Mourning Cloak butterfly.

The sounds of birds singing arose from the grass and mingled with the blowing sound of air current on grass and water. Here and there, yellow, white and pink flowers peeked out along the creek banks.

The valley was, as it appeared, a peaceful place and for someone longing for such a home site, it was near heaven itself. It had been surveyed and marked and now the new owner sat her large horse and spied up the creek for as far as she could see. The sun climbed over her shoulder and cast a thin shadow across the edge of the water. She eased Balloch up on the bank and moved him westward away from the stagecoach road, the last sign of civilization.

Her newly built cabin lay a hundred or more yards from the road and due to the slight curvature of the land only the pitched roof was visible from the thoroughfare. She was in no hurry to return to the one sign of man's presence in the valley but allowed her eyes and even her inner eye to take in the marvel that was now hers.

Buffalo Creek formed one of the semi-perfect valleys just a day's travel to the northeast of the city of Cheyenne. It was a small creek by comparison to others but the water ran downhill and fed the plain and greened the earth. Tall grasses supported the banks and in early summer their seed pods waved in the wind. There seemed to always be the wind. More or less but seldom none.

Birds darted here and there, catching flying insects above the slight current of Buffalo Creek and occasionally diving into the tall grass for something more substantial. Here and there caddis flies escaped the surface tension of the creek and took to the air. Dimpled water provided evidence of feeding trout.

Isla McNeese, lately from Denver, surveyed the grassy slope along Buffalo Creek. She could hardly believe the dream of her own personal Wyoming Territory homestead had come true and not much more than twenty-five miles from one of the fastest growing cities in the west, Cheyenne. She was the first female homesteader in the area and a formidable woman in more ways than one.

Isla was an immigrant from Scotland who had married not long after coming to the United States. Her married name was Hudson, but after months of continuous beatings from her husband, she obtained a divorce and fled to the Tidewater country of lower Virginia and North Carolina. She took back her maiden name, McNeese.

She later brought her knowledge of cattle and her citizenship study book to Colorado and then as a final stop, to Cheyenne. She worked as a cook for six years along the way to support herself, and she saved her money. She was Scottish and neither needed nor wanted much beyond her daily bread. With a year to go of her seven years toward U.S. citizenship, she claimed her homestead northeast of Cheyenne on Buffalo Creek.

Though it was not a large creek, she knew it had enough flow to provide water for a large number of cattle. It was Isla's dream to have a small, self-sustaining ranch with a few head of livestock and the various staples of life. The creek was in all detail, ideal. What Isla did not know was that on the north and south sides of her homestead were two large cattle ranches whose owners were using Buffalo Creek to water their livestock.

They had been watering their cattle at the creek near the ford for close to five years. For some reason, neither of the two ranchers had ever bothered to buy the land on either side of the creek. That was a mistake, but mistakes are made and consequences though unwanted, occur. The creek now belonged to a woman from Scotland and that made all the difference.

Bordering the north side of her homestead was another small homestead parcel similar to her own. She had wished there was some way to add it to her property, but before she could pursue such a course, someone moved onto the land and started their own homestead.

Isla waited a week after her cabin was finished and decided it was time to meet her neighbors and let them know who she was. She saddled the large chestnut gelding she had named Balloch and rode across the creek, crossing the remainder of her land up to the temporary shelter that was undergoing construction by the new homesteaders. She was wearing a leather vest under a tan riding coat though it was not particularly cool weather. Her hands were in leather gloves and a large Stetson crowned her head.

She did not wish to look like a tenderfoot nor an Easterner out of place. The clothes, the horse and her own physical appearance denied any such speculation. She now considered herself a businesswoman rather than a day laborer and she was ready to play the part.

Two men were busy laying a foundation for a medium-sized building. They appeared to be about ten years apart in age, but even a slight observation of their features would have declared them to be brothers. The older-looking one was also the tallest. His hair was long and he had tied it with rawhide to keep it out of his face. Their work clothes were well worn, and it was obvious this was not the labor either of them had foreseen in their move west.

Both men looked up from their digging when Isla rode up on her large horse. They were obviously not in favor of halting their labors but etiquette demanded that they do so. The brothers stopped their work and stared at the imposing visitor. Isla did not dismount. They did not speak but openly gave her the opportunity to say something if that was her desire.

In addition to the rarity of a female visitor, neither of the brothers had ever seen a woman as tall as Isla, although it was hard to estimate how tall she really was sitting on such a large horse and wearing a high-crowned hat. Not only was Isla tall, she was also a fully developed woman and, as such, made an imposing figure. She was not heavy, nor did she seem out of proportion, she was just a large attractive woman. It would be later when they saw her standing on the ground in her heeled boots, that they discovered that she was taller than the oldest brother by two inches, which put her slightly over six feet tall.

"Good morning, neighbors," she said from her superior height on the chestnut. "My name is Isla McNeese, and I'm homesteading the property south of you."

Both men were surprised at the melodious alto tone of her voice. They had expected a deeper and perhaps rougher vocal range. The brothers had to suppress a grin at Isla's thick Scottish brogue though her words were perfectly understandable. They were also taken aback by Isla's large and honest smile. The younger sibling was caught in a fit of embarrassment, and so it was left up to the older one to respond.

"Good morning to you, ma'am. My name is Franklin Jamison, and this young fellow is my brother, Alexander. That's a fine horse you've got there, Miss McNeese."

"Thank you. He can cover some ground. Are you gentlemen building a house this close to the stagecoach road?"

"No, ma'am. We're building a place for travelers to stop and refresh themselves. We also plan on stocking other items as well. You know, things for the local ranchers and workers to relieve them of the long trip to Cheyenne. We plan on raising our own vegetables, chickens and beef."

"I see. Well, I wish you luck. I pretty much plan on doing the same thing as to food and such. Do you know the rancher north of you by any chance?"

"No, ma'am. We just got here three days ago. You're the first person we've met other than some folks headed toward Cheyenne. From the way they're pouring into the Territory, we're going to have a large city near us and in a hurry."

"I see. Well, I plan on making their acquaintance. I think it's good to know who your neighbors are. It's nice to meet you both, Franklin and Alexander Jamison," she paused, "do you have a stove set up yet?"

"No, ma'am, and please call us Frank and Alex. We hope to be good neighbors and friends as well."

"I will do that, Frank, and you gentlemen should just call me Isla. I do have a stove set up, and I would like to invite the two of you for supper tonight. I want to make sure you know where my homestead is. The day might well come when one of us may need the other."

The Jamison brothers accepted the invitation, and after a little more small talk, Isla turned the gelding and headed northeast up the stagecoach road. She did not get very far before she found a trace leading up a slight rise. A large wooden sign with the words

"Rocking AB" hung between two tall poles set on either side of the trace. Sitting on a tall horse and being tall herself, she caught a glimpse of a large roof long before the house itself came into view. It was the largest house she had seen since coming into the Territory, outside of the hotel in Cheyenne.

The broad-winged house was flanked by corrals, and behind the corrals were various buildings. Here and there, she could see figures moving about, some on foot and some on horseback. She had barely hit level ground before two large dogs came flying down the trace from the house. Both dogs were barking ferociously as they closed the distance. She stopped her horse, afraid of what would happen if the dogs got too close. The chestnut had large hooves, and his legs carried a powerful kick.

She remained still and watched the oncoming dogs. Suddenly, a loud, shrill whistle penetrated the distance between the dogs and the house. The dogs stopped in their tracks but continued to bark. On the porch stood a large older man, a rifle held lightly in his right arm. He called out to the dogs, his voice loud and rough, "Come here, you Sam. Come here, you Buff."

The dogs reluctantly withdrew, their hackles raised and their fangs showing down their long jowls. The gentleman with the rifle strode towards Isla and ordered the dogs to stay when he passed by them. He had left the house in a hurry as the absence of a head covering attested. His dark hair was over his ears and a little curly, and his upper lip was partially hidden by a thick handlebar mustache. His face showed frown lines as if to give testimony to a man of few smiles.

He wore black dress pants with a deep brown leather coat, which unbuttoned, showed black suspenders over a white dress shirt. The leather coat had not come cheap. His boots were also of quality and glowed with a deep shine. Isla did not need a second look to know this was a wealthy man in front of her and a large and rich ranch she was riding on. She was surprised at that fact as she had thought all the larger cattle ranches were southeast of Cheyenne in the direction of Muddy Creek. Obviously, she was wrong.

The rancher stopped several feet in front of her and shaded his eyes to see her better. A surprised look flashed across his face when he realized he was talking to a woman, though she was dressed in cowman clothes.

"This is private property, madam. State your business and be on your way. We're busy and don't have time for sightseers."

If the rancher expected a frightened female, he was greatly disappointed. Isla came from strong roots and hardworking people. She did not frighten easily. She tried a pleasant smile.

She was about to speak when the front door of the ranch house opened and a nearly grown teenage girl with long curly hair stepped out onto the porch.

Isla asked, "Is this young lady your daughter, sir?"

"That young lady is none of your business, miss. Now, why are you on my land?"

"Excuse my intrusion, sir. I'm new in the area and wanted to meet my neighbors. My name is Isla McNeese, and I live just past the homestead south of you."

"On the other side of the creek?"

"Not exactly. My house is across the creek, but my homestead includes both sides of the creek. Franklin and Alexander Jamison live on the homestead between you and me."

"What? What did you just say?" The rancher's question was accompanied by his taking three steps forward. His face turned a shade darker, and he sputtered something between the handlebars of the bushy mustache.

"Your homestead is on both sides of the creek? No, miss, that won't do. That won't do at all."

"Well, Mr. ...?"

"Bartram. August Bartram. How much do you want for your place? I'll pay you twice what it's worth. But you cannot have both sides of the creek. We water our cattle there."

"Well, Mr. Bartram, as I was about to say, my homestead is, in fact, on both sides of the creek, and so it will have to do because that is the way it is. I've waited years to get this place, and I'm certainly not going to sell it just because you think it won't do. It actually does fine. Better than fine. I love it just like it is, and soon I'll have cattle of my own on the place. It may not be a fine spread like yours, but it'll suit me. What's your problem anyway?"

"I run a large ranch, Miss McNeese, with over a thousand head of cattle, and Buffalo Creek is our main source of water. We've shared it with the Bar G for over five years now, and we have no interest in that changing."

"I see. Well, to get to the creek, if you go southwest, you'll have to cross the Jamison place and then half of mine. I'm not sure how the Jamisons will feel about that, but I know how I feel. Once I get a few head of cattle, I plan to fence them in, so you will need to find another water source."

"There is no other suitable watering source within five miles of here. "I'll pay you three times your homestead's value, but you cannot, I repeat, cannot stay on Buffalo Creek."

"I'm not selling so there's no need in your offering. Perhaps if we sat down and discussed this, we could come up with a satisfactory solution for all of us. Maybe the Jamisons would grant you access across the western portion of their property, and I could leave a small portion of the creek bank unfenced on that section."

"You put up a fence to keep my cattle out of that creek, I'll have your fence pulled down and the wire destroyed. It will get really expensive for you. There'll be no fences on Buffalo Creek. Do you understand me?"

"I may be a woman, Mr. Bartram, but I'm not afraid of you or your ranch hands. I have a rifle, and I know how to use it. Do you understand me?"

"You're begging for trouble, lady. Out here we take care of problems and problem makers like you, ourselves."

"I came in peace, but you have treated me rudely. I won't come back until you change your attitude and you should not, I repeat, should not trespass on my homestead without asking permission, Mr. Bartram. Good day, sir!"

Anger rising in posture and voice, Isla turned Balloch and spurred him back over the rise and down to the road. It was good her back was turned to rancher Bartram, or she would have seen him sight her in with his Winchester. She rode hard to where she had met the Jamisons, allowing her anger to dissipate as much as possible.

Bartram watched until Isla was out of sight and then turned to go back into his ranch house. His daughter was still waiting on the porch when he arrived. She was full of questions and began asking as soon as her father stepped onto the porch.

"Who was that lady, Daddy?"

"Said her name was Isla McNeese. What kind of name is that? Her speech was so thick I barely understood her."

"Sounds Scottish. Is she from Scotland? She sure is tall. I bet she's the tallest woman in Wyoming, maybe in the west."

"She's a problem, that's what she is. A problem that's got to be solved."

"Where does she live? Does she live near here? I hope so, I would like another woman to talk to."

"She's homesteaded on Buffalo Creek. Owns both sides of the creek. She owns where we water our livestock. We can't have that!"

"Will she sell us water rights?"

"I didn't ask her. Not going to pay to use flowing water just because she owns the creek banks."

"That means she owns access to the water, correct? What are you going to do?"

"Buy her out or run her out. Whichever she wants."

"What if she doesn't want to sell and refuses to run away, Daddy? She's a woman for God's sake."

"Don't you worry about it, Deloris, I'll take care of it."

"Why did you point your rifle at her, Daddy? You taught me never to point a gun at someone you didn't intend to kill. Do you want to kill her?"

"No, Deloris, it was just a reaction. I got a little upset. Like I always say, please don't worry your young head on ranch business."

"I am going to worry. Ever since mother passed away, you have been a different person. Why are you so angry at everyone and everything? I love you so much, but the past is the past and we still have a lot to live for. Mother would not approve of this kind of talk and you know it."

"I'm going to see Ryan. He needs to know about this development. The two of us should have bought that property years ago. Well, we'll buy it now or take it by force, whichever works, and if someone gets hurt, well..."

Tears filled Deloris' eyes. Her father's words stung. He was definitely not the man she knew as a child growing up. She stayed on the porch, absent-mindedly stroking the two dogs who had gathered around her legs. *As soon as he leaves, I'm going to Buffalo Creek and meet this tall Scottish woman.*

TWO

The Jamison brothers were both in shock when Isla relayed her experience at the Rocking AB. Alex, being the younger of the two and less experienced, immediately began to offer suggestions on how to deal with rancher Bartram. It took Frank several minutes to calm his brother down.

"That man has an army of ranch hands, and there's very little law out here in the Territory. Going up against him with firearms is the last thing we want to do."

"You're right, Frank." Isla said, "You fellows come over before dark, and we'll work on some ideas while we eat."

Isla rode up to her small house and went inside. Moments later, she exited with a Colt on her hip and an old Winchester in her right hand. She would not make the mistake of meeting the owner of the Bar G unarmed. She was disappointed that her meeting with Bartram had turned as sour as it had. The thought that there was no neighbor between her and the Bar G made her even more cautious. Hopefully, the southern rancher was a little more hospitable.

Isla cantered down the stagecoach road towards Cheyenne. She recalled seeing a sign near a small hill that had Bar G Cattle Ranch cut on it. Once she reached the sign, she found a trail through the grass alongside the hill. There was nothing on her side of the hill that blocked her view of the mountains rising in the distant background. No one would miss the spectacular view.

She rode for half a mile before the hill fell away. There to the south lay the Bar G ranch. The house was not as large as the one she had seen earlier, but it was beautiful in its setting. Fruit trees and flowering shrubs surrounded the porch and foundation. The nearest outbuilding was over forty yards behind the house.

Again, Isla saw cowboys and horses. In the distance, close to a small enclosure, she spied a flock of chickens pecking around under the supervision of a rather large red and black rooster. In front of the porch was a whitewashed hitching rail. She rode up to the rail and observed the house. Nothing moved nor gave an alarm. She called out, "Hello, the house," her voice covering the distance and penetrating the wooden door and glass windows. The large front door opened.

Isla uttered an audible sigh. Instead of a blustering rancher, a middle-aged woman opened the door and looked at her. She was wearing her reddish-brown hair in a bun with a large jade pin stuck through it.

She wore a common-looking green dress and low-heeled boots that reached just above her ankles. She was plain and yet at the same time beautiful.

"Hello," she said, "may I help you?"

Isla removed her hat and smiled. Another woman and she wasn't holding a rifle or shotgun. No panting, growling dogs twisted around her feet and the entire atmosphere felt welcoming.

"Ma'am, my name is Isla McNeese. I live just north of you. My homestead lies on both sides of Buffalo Creek. I wanted to meet my neighbors and let you know I'm here."

"Good afternoon, Miss McNeese. I'm Carla Gardener. My husband is Ryan Gardener. We are the owners of the Bar G. I'm sorry Ryan's not here at the moment. Another neighbor just dropped by and the two of them are in the barn or somewhere. Won't you get down and come inside? I have coffee, and usually there is some cake in the safe."

As soon as Deloris' father was out of sight, the young girl went to the stable and saddled her small mare. One of the hands offered to help but she wasn't in the mood for conversation and she had been able to saddle her own horse before she became a teenager. She had not ridden for several days and the mare was a little excited so she urged her into a short run to get the nervous energy down before she headed for the stagecoach road.

Deloris was surprised when she came upon the Jamisons working on their future store. She had no idea that someone had moved in next to them. Her eyes took in the scene and sorted through the picture she saw. Two men, one of them about her age, were sawing and hammering. *The younger one is kinda cute,* she thought. She wondered what their names were and what they were building so close to the road.

The two of them looked up as the sound of her horse on the packed earth reached them. The older of the two went back to sawing, but the younger one stared at her until she was out of sight. That bit of information pleased Deloris but she gave no sign.

Deloris was disappointed when she reached Isla's house to find the lady gone. She so wanted to talk to another female and especially this one who sounded Scottish and was so tall and more importantly, had stood up to her father. She promised to return the next time her father was away from home. Between Isla and the young man who stared at her life had suddenly taken an exciting turn.

Isla's nervousness lessened somewhat, and she quickly dismounted her horse and tied him to the hitching rail.

"I can't stay long; I have guests coming for supper. I was hoping to meet your husband, Mr. Gardener."

"I'm sure he'll be finished in a few minutes. He'll have word that you're here, and he will not want to miss you."

True enough, Ryan Gardener was hearing August Bartram's version of his earlier confrontation with Isla McNeese when informed by a stable hand of her arrival at his ranch. Ryan was interested in meeting the woman who fit the description he had just heard from his ranching friend.

"Let me talk to her, A.B., and see what she has to say before we do anything rash. We may save a lot of trouble and energy by just waiting a bit. Sometimes these things have a way of taking care of themselves. She may tire of homesteading in a few weeks and be happy to make a small profit on her place, and our troubles will be over."

"I'm not much on waiting, Ryan. These things can get out of hand. Best to tackle it head-on and get it over with. Less pain that way. I say let's buy her out or run her off. We've got plenty of help. Stampedes, fire, lots of things can happen around ranches."

"Okay, but before we go to extremes, let me size her up. Maybe I can get off on a better foot than you did. Can't see as how it could be much worse."

Ten minutes later, Ryan walked into the kitchen and found the woman he and August had been discussing sitting and drinking coffee with his wife. He had never really thought of Carla as being short as a woman, even though she was three or four inches shorter than he was. He had been warned but seeing a woman that tall was still a surprise. Isla McNeese, his water-access-owning neighbor, was a very tall woman.

Isla long ago had learned the value of standing as tall as or taller than those who wanted to misuse her in some way. She immediately set her cup down and rose to her feet. She offered her hand to Ryan, who took it and bowed.

Carla introduced Isla to Ryan and then Ryan to Isla.

"Please sit back down, Miss McNeese," Ryan said, his face perfectly at ease.

"Thank you, Mr. Gardener, but I've already overstayed my time. I just wanted to meet you and let you know you have a new neighbor."

"We thank you, Miss McNeese. Delighted to meet you and have you in the area. I hear you homesteaded the land on both sides of Buffalo Creek. Is that right?"

"I see Mr. Bartram got here before I did. Yes, the creek splits the homestead from west to east. My property ends at the stagecoach road."

"Yes, yes, he came with the news. Just left, actually. Seemed all worried that you were going to put the two of us out of business and ruin our lives. Is that your plan, miss?"

"No, but I'm not too keen on being bullied or threatened, Mr. Gardener, and Mr. Bartram tried both on me."

"What?" Carla cried out.

"And you intend to raise a few head of stock, I believe?" Ryan asked, ignoring his wife's interruption.

"Yes, enough to make a living anyway."

"Mr. Bartram seems to have the idea that you are going to control water access and deny its benefit to the two of us. Is that the plan?"

"No. It's not the plan. There isn't much of a plan, actually. I will fence in part of the creek for my cattle and personal use. I made no other particulars."

"Oh, no! Ryan, he didn't..." Carla finally got out.

"I'm afraid he did, dear, but he'll settle down. I'm sure of it. I told him to give Miss McNeese time. I am sure we can work something out.

"Miss McNeese, did you forbid Mr. Bartram from trespassing on your land?"

"Yes, I did, after he threw me off of his ranch and told me not to come back. Seems like fair is fair to me. And, to answer your question, Mr. Gardener, I do plan on having a small herd of cattle and other livestock. There is plenty of water, and I am sure we can work out an agreement that satisfies us all."

Carla attempted to explain the situation to Isla, she stood up and halfway reached for Isla's hand.

"A.B. is not himself, not the man he was before Eloise, his wife, passed away. She had a heart attack and died suddenly. It shocked A.B. and changed him. He has never accepted her death, blaming God and the world in general for what happened. He was left with that little girl...well, she's not so little anymore...to raise, and she and that ranch are all he cares about. Maybe he'll come around. Ryan and I will talk to him."

"It'll take some change, that's for sure," Isla said.

Isla nodded a quick thank you to Carla and then stepped to the door. Before leaving, she paused for a moment and looked slightly down at Ryan Gardener.

"I'm from the Highlands of Scotland, sir, and we treat our neighbors fairly and right. But so you and your rancher friend understand, we are not so kind to those who make themselves our enemies."

Isla gently closed the door behind her and mounted her horse. By the time Ryan had recovered and made it through the door, her retreating back was yards down the entry trace.

THREE

The days slipped by, and nothing was heard from the Rocking AB. Isla and the Jamisons were unaware that the ranch's cattle were farther north in a hilly area but would be brought to the valley when cooler weather came. It was obvious that fall was arriving ahead of schedule. Frank and Alex set up a routine of work and visiting Isla for meals. Slowly, small repairs and additions were made to the McNeese homestead. The three neighbors were fast becoming friends.

Three weeks later, Isla prepared a dish she had learned about while in the Tidewater. She was enjoying the company of the two brothers, and they were enjoying the excellent meals and Isla's conversation.

Frank and Alex worked unabashedly on their second bowl of the special chicken dish Isla had served them for supper. Their relish for the dish either attested to its goodness or to the nature of their own cooking, or both.

"This is really good, Miss McNeese. I've never tasted anything like it before. What's it called?" Alex asked.

"It's called chicken bog in the Tidewater country, and in other places, a dish like it is called chicken 'perlo,'" Isla answered. "And, please, call me Isla. Remember, we're going to be friends as well as neighbors."

Frank joined in the conversation, "What's in this besides chicken and rice?"

"Oh, a little of this and a little of that, you know, some leftover onions, dried celery, spices, and of course bacon flavor. If you like it fresh-made, just wait till you've had it as leftovers.

"Do you and Alex have family back east?"

"No, our parents were killed by a marauding band of Union soldiers raiding the eastern part of Missouri where our home place was. I was in the war, not far from Shiloh, Tennessee when it happened. Alex was in a small one-room schoolhouse that the raiders missed.

"When the war ended, I found Alex living with a neighbor who was somehow spared in the raid. Our farm was completely ravaged and the memories were just too strong for us to stay there. We went west to Nebraska and then saw fliers about free land in the Wyoming Territory and so we came here. I had some money saved up from the war and we decided on making a brand-new start.

"We didn't plan on fighting cattle barons or meeting someone like you. How did a Scottish lady wind up being our southern neighbor?"

"I came to America about seven years ago. I started out in Boston because there were jobs for women due to all the Irishmen arriving. I should have known that Irishmen were not good neighbors for Scots. I moved south to New York and got a job as an assistant cook in the city. That's where I met Ranson Hudson. I married him mostly for security but it turned out that I was worse off than before the wedding. He had a terrible temper and I got the wrong end of it.

"I found a young lawyer who helped me to divorce him. It's very hard to do in New York but somehow it happened. I fled the city and went to the Tidewater area of Virginia and then the Carolinas. Those are some strange people, although they were very kind to me. Of course, they made fun of my accent and height. My experience with Ranson made me swear I would never let a man treat me that way again.

"I heard about the west, especially Denver, Colorado, so I took the train west. I stopped here and there and worked and when I had enough money, I bought another ticket west.

"When I arrived in Denver, I got a full-time job as a cook in one of the largest restaurants in the city. It paid good and I lived cheap and saved my money. I spent my time off studying to become an American citizen.

"I kept hearing stories about Cheyenne and Wyoming. I read a bulletin about free homesteads in the area and so when I thought I had enough money, I headed for Cheyenne to find my Promised Land. I wanted a place with running water and good grass. I knew from our cattle in the Highlands that cows drink a lot of water. I still can't believe I was so lucky to find Buffalo Creek. This valley should be called Paradise."

Frank finished his second helping and shoved his plate closer to the center of the small round table they were seated at. He also gave a sigh of complete satisfaction.

"Miss Isla, if you want to go back to cooking, you could surely work for Alex and me once we get our restaurant open."

"Well, thank you, Frank. I consider that a compliment. I'll certainly keep it in mind. I don't want to keep you men too long, but I am interested in hearing what you have to say about our neighbors."

"I didn't bring Alex out here to get in a new war, and I had enough of the last one to last me a lifetime. I also don't intend to get bullied, either. Alex and I want to run a few head of steers for resale, and they will need water. We're willing to compensate you fairly for the use of the creek on the side where it backs up against us. To be honest, I hate to get involved in a neighbor's business."

"What if they pull you into it?" Isla asked.

"I don't know. I guess we'll have to decide if it's worth it or not. We really don't have much to say about your border with the Bar G."

"That's true, but I think whatever Bartram does will have some influence on Gardener. Gardener is a businessman and thinks like one; Bartram is a bully and thinks like one. I just wish we had a marshal or sheriff or some kind of lawman out in the country."

Frank changed the subject, moving away from the growing water saga. "Isla, I noticed your cabin is small and not too tight. Cold weather is coming. When Alex and I finish our buildings would you be interested in swapping labor? We would help finish this building and help with some others in exchange for your cooking lunch and supper for us. We'd throw in some food, too."

Isla looked around the walls and corners of her small house. It was true that while she was handy with a saw and hammer, erecting the house by herself had been difficult. She had regretted letting the older man who had helped with the stove and furniture go. It was foolish pride, really. Here was a chance to rectify the mistake and avoid being totally alone during the winter. She was aware that the news of a single woman living alone would circulate among the ranch hands and drifters in the area, and while cowhands tended to be protective of women, you couldn't be sure a bad one wouldn't come along.

"I think the answer is yes. Let me consider it in detail for a few days. How long do you think it will be before your buildings are finished?"

"If our next delivery of lumber and supplies comes in the next few days, we should finish in another week or two. Oh, one other thing. I noticed you have chickens. When you have some extra laying hens, we would like to purchase a few."

"You homesteaded without any fowl?"

"We had two hens, but something ate them before we could build a pen. Probably coyotes. This time we'll build the pen first."

Isla smiled. It felt good to smile, and after the gentlemen left, she found herself humming as she cleared up the dishes. There was plenty of the chicken bog left, and her new friends would be returning to finish it off at lunchtime the next day.

The sun broke through early morning clouds, its beams striking the lone window at the front of Isla's small house, throwing light into the interior. Isla was behind the house scattering some scraps for her brood of hens. She had let the rooster out of the pen first, to do some bug hunting on his own. She wished she had some mangelwurzel but there had been none available where she bought the fowl. She intended on planting it in the spring and some greens as well. Her family had sworn by greens for chickens.

Once the hens were fed, she would open their gate as well. Even with a large rooster, no brood of hens or flock of chickens was safe from the hawks, foxes, and coyotes. What she needed, she realized, was a dog. Not just for the livestock when she acquired them, but to warn her of unwelcomed guests as well. She added a guard dog to her list of needs.

Isla came around the side of the small frame house, wiping her hands on her apron and pushing a stray lock of hair off her forehead. She scanned the horizon for a sign of rain clouds and nodded at the lack of any. It would be a cooler but clear day; she was certain of that. Perhaps a day to finish the root cellar she had begun three days earlier. It had to be deeper than the frost line to keep the vegetables from freezing and the milk from souring.

"Milk," she said out loud though there was no one there but herself. "I need a cow, like yesterday. I can't go to Gardener's, and I won't go to Bartram's. Probably be best to head towards Cheyenne as there are more ranches that way." Isla removed the apron and hung it on a nail beside the front door. Next, she removed the tack from a small rack in her bedroom and went back outside to catch her horse. She saddled up Balloch and started up the road towards the Jamisons'. She might as well see if they needed anything since she was going.

She stopped her mount short of their building project and shaded her steel-blue eyes. Far in the distance, she could see movement on the vague roadway. She held her horse still and waited. A glance at the neighbors confirmed that they were hard at work and had not noticed her approach. She was surprised at the speed with which their main building was coming together.

Whatever was on the road was not in a hurry and she found herself nervous and curious at the same time. She glanced again at the Jamisons and urged Balloch forward at a steady trot. As the gap closed between her and the movement ahead, she was sure it was a herd of cattle being driven down the road towards her. Several riders were now visible and she was sure she saw smaller animals darting here and there. She also realized she was approaching Bartram's ranch and with that knowledge came the animosity she had felt the day before. She pulled her horse up short and waited.

Isla could make out the cattle as they drew closer and she could also see that the smaller animals were black and white dogs moving on the outskirts of the cattle. Occasionally, one would dart in on a drifting steer and snap at its legs, causing the steer to veer back to the moving herd. She counted four horsemen in the rear and on the sides. She wondered how many animals were in the herd; there were a lot, she was sure of that.

One of the riders saw her and broke around the herd and rode up to where she was sitting. He tipped his hat as he looked her over.

"Excuse me, ma'am, but we would like to get these beeves on to Cheyenne. If you could move up off the roadway, it would be helpful."

"Certainly, cowboy. May I ask you a question?"

"Surely, ma'am. Bill Langley at your service."

"Nice to meet you, Mr. Langley. My name is Isla McNeese. What are you doing with the cattle, moving or selling?"

"We are taking them to Cheyenne to sell. Why are you asking?"

"I'm looking for a cow to milk and a few cows to start a herd with."

"We've got a few cows; Cookie's been milking one or two of them for making biscuits and what-not. I'll check with the boss and see what he says. I don't think it matters much to him whether we sell the whole bunch in Cheyenne or on the way."

That unexpected but pleasant piece of business concluded, Isla sat in the middle of the road, twenty cows and one small tan wirehaired dog in front of her. The cattle drive was almost out of sight. She smiled as she looked over her new purchases. She was watching the young dog moving around his charges and failed to hear the riders' approach behind her.

"You starting a dairy?" a voice called out behind her back. She spun her head around to see who it was, although she thought she recognized the voice. The question was followed by laughter from the four riders behind August Bartram.

Isla did not respond, at least not with words, but her face was answer enough for the cowhands. Bartram just smiled, satisfied at his insult and the reaction he had caused, too self-centered to realize he had made a serious enemy. He was not the first male to underestimate the opposite sex. Heat rose up Isla's neck but it wasn't from embarrassment. She held her anger in, knowing it was not the place or time for confrontation.

The new cattle owner urged her horse forward, calling on the dog to move the cows ahead of her. Getting the cattle dog was an extra bonus she was quite pleased with. The herders had offered to throw in the smaller dog, who was obviously different from the black and white ones they were using. The cowboy who brought her the cows offered that the dog was a stray that had taken up with them but had learned to work the cattle by watching the other dogs. They didn't need him but hadn't run him off either. The animal came without a name, but the cowboy said the hands just called him Dog. Since he answered to that, she used it, thinking she might give him a name later.

Dog barked and snapped at a few heels and the cows began lumbering down the road toward Isla's homestead. Suddenly, Bartram and his men pushed past Isla and into the small herd, scattering them off the road, and causing some of them to run in the opposite direction. Isla could hear the men laughing as they moved down the road and out of sight. She reached for her rifle, but changed her mind. She realized that they were trying to get her goat and make her say or do something foolish. She clenched her teeth and spurred her horse to help Dog reassemble the cows and resume their trip to the homestead.

In a few minutes, the cattle drive drew abreast of the homestead of Frank and Alex Jamison. Isla had planned to stop and show the two men her newly purchased cows, but she only paused for a second. Bartram and his men were sitting their horses just a few feet from where the two brothers were working. She could tell a heated argument was underway and she guessed the nature of it. The Jamisons were no more likely to sell than she was. Bartram now had two homesteads between him and the creek to worry about. *How much force would he employ?* she wondered.

Isla had a feeling that this would not end well, and the feeling caused a slight shudder across her shoulders. She moved on, putting distance between herself and the argument, knowing the brothers would tell her what transpired when they came to lunch. Meanwhile, she needed to get the cows settled across the creek and behind her house. Her thoughts turned to the things she needed to work on that day. She also had a moment to wonder if Dog would take to the chickens and guard them or if he would chase them. She needed the dog to help with the cows, but she needed the chickens as well.

Dog was a big help getting the cows to wade the creek. They were thirsty from their long trail drive so getting them to the water was not hard. However, the grass on the edge of the water was lush and they were satisfied to stay there and graze. Isla hoped they were as reluctant to leave the grass on the other side once they were there. Between her horse and Dog and lots of yelling, the small herd finally waded across and settled in on the grass on the south side of the creek. Isla and the dog drove them upstream and away from the ford at the stagecoach road. She wanted the cows behind her house where she could see them while working outside.

Isla unsaddled her horse and turned him loose with the cows. He and the dog exchanged nose touches and then the gelding began to graze, much more interested in the grass than cows or a dog. Isla walked down towards the chickens, who were busy searching for bugs and seeds and then turned and called for the dog to come. Dog cast a glance at her and then the cows and then back to her again. She called him again and clapped her hands together. Dog trotted over beside her. He stood still as she patted his head, focused on the chickens running here and there more than he was on Isla.

She stopped patting his head and moved to walk through the fowl towards the root cellar she was digging. The dog stood still for a minute and then leaned forward to smell the chickens. The rooster strutted up and flexed his wings and ruffled his feathers. Dog ignored him and basically Isla as well, turning around and trotting back to the cows. He had accepted his responsibility and declared his intentions to work at the homestead. Isla smiled and went about her task.

Dog looked like he had some Airedale Terrier blood mixed with who knew what. Though the Airedales originated in Yorkshire, England, many were found in Scotland. She knew the Terrier breed well but how one got to America was a mystery. Perhaps an immigrant had brought one or a crossbreed of some kind. He was small to be a pure Airedale Terrier but he showed some of the breed's temperament in addition to color and wirehair. He wasn't too old, Isla observed, and maybe he would grow a little larger. Anyway, he knew his business and took care of it and that made Isla feel very lucky to have him.

When the sun neared the middle of the sky, she dropped her shovel and picked up a bucket, and headed for the creek. Her neighbors would be arriving soon and she wanted to get lunch warming on the stove. She needed water for washing up and for the large pot of coffee she knew would be needed. She thought of having company and the unhappy thoughts Bartram's presence had caused were replaced with the happiness of having friends coming to visit. She would not have to eat alone and that in itself made her happy.

Back in the cabin, Isla built a small fire in the wood cook stove and put the water on to boil. While the water heated, she got out the things they would need for lunch. She wished she had made a pie or cake, but she had just been too busy. Besides, if they were going to eat with her every day, she couldn't afford cakes and pies at all meals.

Once the water was warm, she took a cloth and a small piece of soap and washed her face and hands, then she found her brush and a small mirror and made herself as attractive as possible. She convinced herself that she was just doing what civilized women did when entertaining guests, men or women.

"You're not looking for a husband, Isla," she said to the face in the mirror. The mirror didn't seem convinced and kept silent about it. She started the coffee and then busied herself straightening and dusting her few possessions in the living/kitchen area. She was unaware of the arrival of her guest until Dog gave the alarm. She stepped outside the door and called him over to her. He had left the cows to intervene with the arriving brothers. She was extremely pleased to know that the dog had decided that this was his place and that he stood ready to guard it. She would introduce Frank and Alex before she sent him back out to the cows.

Frank led the way and when he reached the door, he dropped to one knee and held out the back of his hand towards the dog. Dog reached his nose out and sniffed Frank's hand but his tail did not move and his hair was still up on his back. Alex went to step around Frank and greet Isla but was immediately met with low growls and bared fangs. Isla leaned down and stroked Dog's head and ears. She talked in a slow and soft voice. Frank kept his hand out and Alex backed up. Slowly Dog's hackles lowered and the snarls disappeared.

Frank talked softly and held his palm open. Again, Dog reached out with his nose and smelled the hand.

Frank held steady, making sure he did not make sudden movements. Dog took one short step towards the two men and stopped. He touched Frank's hand with his tongue and when Frank didn't move, Dog eased back.

"Where did he come from?" Frank asked.

"I got him along with some cows from a herd that went by this morning."

"Yeah, we saw them," Alex said.

"Didn't see you, though," Frank said, "we were being hounded by your friends, Bartram and his crew."

Isla pointed towards the cows with her right hand and held Dog's scruff with her left. "Go, Dog, guard the cattle," she said and half pushed him toward the herd. Dog looked at Frank and Alex one last time and then began to run towards the small herd of cows.

"Sorry about that, gentlemen. I had no idea he would react that way. Come on in before he changes his mind. I want to hear about your visit with Bartram and his armed guards."

The two men took seats at the table while Isla poured three cups of coffee and put the chicken bog on the stove to warm. There was no cream or sugar on the table but homesteaders were used to drinking their coffee black. Isla brushed a stray hair from her face and sat down opposite Frank.

"What'd he offer for your place?" Isla asked.

"First, he just wanted free access across our land, and grazing rights as well. We argued a while and he got a little riled. He offered to buy the homestead and pay us for the work we have done already but I told him no, because we have plans for the place. Then he offered me twice what the place was worth. I said no again. So, he said if that was the way it was, he would just come over anyway and we could just take it as he wasn't going to argue with me, or, he said, that woman on the other side of you."

Isla said an unladylike word and got up from her chair to dip the bog into three plain white bowls. She also put a tray with homemade bread in the middle of the table. No butter yet of course.

"I think he's just bluster," Alex said.

"No, Alex, I think he's a mean man. Anyone who would treat a woman the way he's treated me has little in the way of scruples," Isla replied.

"We'll know pretty soon, I'm certain of that," Frank said.

"What do you mean, Frank?" Isla asked.

"He's not going to let this fester and because he's used to bullying people to get his way, he will act to intimidate us. He'll try to get his way or force us to leave or fight."

"Well, I'm not selling and I'm not leaving so I guess it's fight for me," Isla said.

"Isn't there any law around here?" Alex asked.

"Sure, there's a sheriff in Cheyenne. We're too far away and these guys are too rich for the sheriff to bother. He probably believes in open range and no water rights," Frank answered.

All three were temporarily caught up in their own thoughts as they ate the delicious chicken bog. For several minutes it was quiet in the small living area. Finally, all three were finished. Isla stood up to gather the dishes. Frank also stood up and cleared his throat.

"That was better than yesterday, Isla, and I didn't think that possible. Alex and I will bring the fixings for supper and while you cook, the two of us will make some improvements to your house, if that's suitable to you."

"Thank you, Frank, Alex; that will be nice. I hate to say it, but you two might need to start wearing firearms while you work or at least have them nearby. I don't trust Bartram any further than I do an Irishman."

"You might better keep a rifle close, yourself," Alex said.

"I plan to."

FOUR

That afternoon, Isla moved furniture to make room for her carpenters and then resumed her digging of the root cellar. The chickens scratched in the grass, watched over by the large rooster, and the cows and Balloch slowly ate their way towards the creek under the watchful eye of Dog. Isla's Winchester leaned against the wooden side of the chicken house, a few feet from where she was working. Aside from its ominous presence, the scene could well have come from a flyer about the wonderful life in the Wyoming Territory.

The afternoon passed without incident and soon Isla looked up from her work, realizing that it was growing darker. The sun was almost to the mountaintop on the southwest horizon. She jumped with a start as she remembered that she had a cow to milk. The rancher had been kind enough to give her one cow that had recently freshened and she was eager to see how much milk she would get. She would be able to use all of it as there was no calf to share with.

It also occurred to her that she had not provided a place to hold the cow while she milked it. That could be a problem. She got a pan and a pail from the kitchen shelf and carried them out behind the chicken house. The chickens were already making their way into their pen for the evening roost. Isla put a couple of handfuls of corn in the pan and set it down near the corner of the outbuilding. Taking a length of rope, she headed for the small herd and the brown and white cow whose udder was almost dragging the ground.

As needy as the cow was, Isla wondered if she would have caught her on foot without Dog. She decided that Maggie, her name for the milking cow, needed a halter with a short catch rope attached. Between she and Dog and her throw rope, Maggie finally made it to the shed where Isla tied her up, sort of. Once Maggie saw the corn, she settled down long enough to eat. Isla managed to hang on to Maggie's moving hind quarters enough to almost fill the gallon pail. Not near as much as the dairy cows she had known back in Scotland but enough for her purpose and surprisingly, the butterfat seemed as high. She would know as soon as the milk was separated.

Isla took the raw milk and set it in the deepest part of the partially dug cellar and covered it with several layers of cloth to keep it clean and out of the sun. There was not enough time left before supper to make butter but the cream would rise to the top before she went to bed.

Maggie was set loose, a small catch rope tied to a quickly made rope harness. Isla decided she needed to give the dog a real name. She once had a Scotty named Roy. She liked the sound of it and it was a good Scottish name. Maggie and the newly named Roy hurried back to the small herd, Maggie to graze and Roy to herd. Isla went into the house and retrieved two pitchers, which she filled at the edge of the stream. She had no idea what the Jamisons were bringing for supper but she was sure water would be needed. She needed to make coffee anyway.

Isla filled the coffee pot with water and began mixing dough for biscuits. She found she was humming to herself again and feeling relaxed for the first time in a long time. The light in the window on the south side grew dimmer and she was surprised when she heard Roy bark and the sound of horse hooves.

The main room of the cabin was soon full of food, tools, lumber and a bucket of mud. Frank and Alex were both eager to share the items they had brought for the supper and commenced to talk at once. Isla broke into laughter and held up her hand.

"Wait, wait, fellows. One at a time, please. Alex, you go first."

"Well, there's some cured venison from a deer I shot a few days ago. There are a few potatoes from our last trip to town and a jar of molasses for biscuits...you making biscuits, right?"

"Yes, I'm making biscuits. When spring comes, we'll have to make a large garden for fresh vegetables to put up for the summer and fall. I've started a root cellar and it should be finished before frost. I've got some fresh milk in the low end of it right now. Enough for a glass for each of us and some to make butter in the morning. By lunch, we can have butter with our leftover biscuits."

Frank lowered the bag he had slung over his shoulder and removed a small metal tool.

"I'm starting on mudding some of these cracks and holes. It'll be a little warmer come the first freeze."

Alex picked up another bag and some boards and headed for the door. "I'll get started on the outbuildings while you do that, big brother."

"Say," Isla chimed in, "could you fix a milking stanchion on the back side of the chicken house? I need to be able to hold the cow still while I milk her. A food trough below the stanchion would be helpful."

"I never built one before but it shouldn't be too hard."

"Just a minute. I have a drawing I made for myself. Something like it would serve just fine."

Isla went back to her efforts at biscuits and the rest of the supper. In the relative quietness, she heard Frank humming under his breath. It was a pleasant tune that she recognized and she quietly added her voice to his. Each was aware of the other, but neither spoke, content for the sharing of the moment and growing friendship.

When Frank and Alex rose to leave, Isla said, "Why don't the two of you come for breakfast in the morning? There will be fresh milk and maybe some butter."

"Sounds wonderful. Fresh milk and butter on your biscuits. How can we say no?" Alex answered.

The sun and Isla rose close to the same time, Isla beating it by a few minutes. Her first chore was to retrieve the milk she had left in the unfinished root cellar. Using a large spoon, she carefully skimmed the rich cream off of the top of the pail and put it in a medium-sized jar. The leftover milk went back to the cellar, but the jar of cream was left on the table in the middle of the room.

Next came feeding the chickens and then milking the cow. She was anxious to try the new stanchion Alex had built the evening before. She fed the chickens and turned them loose. Isla gathered the eggs, happy to find there were enough for the three diners to have two eggs each. She put grain in the trough just below the stanchion and opened the stanchion. She called Roy, who was lying down near the cows, watching her pour out the grain but keeping an eye on the cattle.

Isla sent Roy after Maggie. Maggie was a name she remembered from her youth. An older lady who lived near her family's farm whom she often took butter and eggs to in exchange for a little spending money. Maggie had been a little heavy, just like the cow and her hair color was nearly the same shade of brown as the spotted milk cow.

Once rounded up, Maggie had little choice but to follow Isla to the stanchion. Isla had the short rope and Roy was nipping at her heels. The stanchion did its work and Isla finished in half the time of the previous night. She turned Maggie loose, put the milk away, and headed to her kitchen area to start the morning fire and make dough for the biscuits. She made coffee in a large kettle and poured herself a cup. There would be eggs and leftover deer meat to help the biscuits along.

Once those chores were over, Isla examined the jar of cream. The jar felt warm enough to start the butter-making process and so Isla found the jar's lid and screwed it on as tight as she could. She pulled a chair from the small table and sat down with the jar. Between sips of hot coffee, she turned the jar over and over, slightly shaking it in the process. As her cup emptied, the cream became small hunks of butter. Over and over went the jar until very little liquid was left. Isla took the jar to the large pan she used as a sink and pouring water into the jar she washed the lumps of butter out.

She took the lumps and mashed them together, kneading the newly formed lump over and over to remove the buttermilk; she did not want the butter to become rancid too quickly. Satisfied, she molded the butter into a round patty and placed it on a dish. It took all her reserves not to wipe her fingers across the fresh butter and taste it. She and the men would enjoy it with hot biscuits before the hour was finished.

She put the biscuits in the oven and began cracking eggs into a bowl. The quiet morning was shattered by the urgent barking of Roy, mixed with what sounded like low growls and cattle lowing and snorting. She grabbed her rifle with her right hand and her Stetson with her left. She jammed the hat down on her head and yanked the door open to the yard. Roy was standing at the near bank of the creek, the hair on his neck and back raised, and barking loudly at the milling cattle on the north side of the steam.

The trespassing herd was surrounded by mounted cowboys, but on the eastern side of the cattle, three men sat on horseback facing each other. It was obvious they were arguing with much arm pointing and waving. Isla recognized Frank and Alex but the third rider was a stranger to her. She guessed that he was the head wrangler for August Bartram. Isla felt the anger rise from within and fill her head. She ran to her side of the creek bank and fired her rifle in the air.

The unexpected shot got everyone's attention: cows, Roy, cowboys, Frank and Alex and the apparent trail boss. Isla's cows and the unwelcomed cattle all moved into motion though in opposite directions. Roy ran after her cows. The movement of the cattle and the barking of Roy were the only sounds. The startled men sat on their mounts, unsure what to do.

Isla did not hesitate to move the situation forward. She called across the creek, her voice clear in spite of the Scottish brogue.

"You are trespassing! Get those cows and your persons off my property and do it now. I warned your boss not to do this. You've trespassed the Jamisons' property and now you're on mine illegally. Get off before I defend my rights with this rifle."

She saw Frank speak to the trail boss and then he and Alex turned their horses into the creek. The cowboys laughed and the apparent leader called back to her. "Settle down, miss. We'll be gone in a few minutes. There's plenty of water."

"There's plenty of water, but this water is on my property and you have no right being on my property. One last warning: get off my land!"

Frank and Alex reached the south bank and Frank rode up to Isla. "Let it be for now, Isla. There are more of them than us and this can quickly grow into something ugly. Alex and I will go see Bartram with you after breakfast."

"Yes, I will go see him, but these cattle are leaving now."

Isla raised the rifle and took careful aim. The bullet landed beneath the trail boss's horse. The cattle spooked again and the horse bolted, throwing its rider in the process.

"Next one won't be in the dirt. Now vacate my property and don't come back."

Frank reached for the rifle, but Isla shook him off. "You're not my father or my husband, Frank. Back me or leave but don't interfere in this."

Frank's face turned red and he retreated to his horse. He motioned for Alex to follow him as he led the horse to the front of Isla's cabin. Alex was in shock and kept looking back at Isla who was standing with her rifle raised in the air. Alex glanced at the men on the other side. He breathed a sigh of relief when he saw them pushing the cattle away from the bank and to the north.

Frank went into the house and opened the oven door to check the biscuits. Much longer and they would have been burned. He rescued them and sat them on the table next to the butter. Alex also came in and Frank got two cups and poured them both a cup of coffee. They sat down at the table without speaking, each sipping their coffee and hoping Isla wasn't so angry she wouldn't fix breakfast.

Isla came in the door without saying a word. She put her hat on the peg and leaned the rifle against the doorframe, keeping it within easy reach. Frank and Alex looked at her face and hid their own in their coffee cups. Isla went to work on the eggs, mixing them and adding bits of venison as she did. When she was satisfied, she put the mixture in a large pan and placed the pan on the stovetop. She flipped it over and when it was firm, she cut it into three parts and ladled it onto three plates. These she placed on the table with some authority and a continued silence.

Frank asked, "Do you mind if I say grace?"

Isla shook her head and then bowed it.

When Frank was finished, Isla jumped up from the table and grabbed the pan of biscuits and the jar of butter. She put them in the middle of the table, paused to say something, changed her mind and sat down and began to eat. The rest of the meal was consumed in silence and awkward glances between Frank and Alex. It was a short meal due to lack of conversation.

Frank stood up and carried his plate to the wash pan. He was followed by Alex who started to speak to Isla but held his tongue. He was anxious to find out if the milking stanchion worked satisfactorily. Neither of the two brothers had ever seen a female so angry and didn't have any idea what to do. Frank looked at Alex and nodded towards the door. When they reached it, Frank spoke, keeping his voice soft and low.

"Thank you for a delicious meal, Isla."

Isla looked up, acknowledging them for the first time. "The stanchion worked just fine, Alex. I'm sorry for speaking unkindly to you, Frank. Don't forget to bring groceries for lunch."

The two men exited the house and mounted up, keeping their silence until they were headed to the road.

"Whew," Frank said.

"Whew is right," Alex answered.

Halfway home, the two riders saw August Bartram and the cowboy Frank had been talking to coming at a gallop toward them.

"Turn around," Frank yelled, and the two of them spurred their horses into a run for Isla's house. Neither of them took time to tie up their mounts but threw the reins on the ground and pounded on Isla's door.

"What is it?" she called.

"Open up, Isla. Bartram and his hired hand are headed this way in a hurry."

Isla opened the door and stepped out onto the grass, rifle in her right hand but pointed to the ground. Before she could ask any questions, the two approaching horsemen turned from the road towards her front door.

The Jamisons stepped up beside Isla, one on each side of her. Both had taken their revolvers from their saddlebags and placed them in their belts. While neither brother was an expert with handguns, both were familiar enough to use them if necessary. They were nervous but tried not to show it because Isla appeared so calm and collected.

It was how she appeared but not how she felt. She had come to Wyoming to live her dream and the dream had not included neighbor versus neighbor arguments and certainly not violence of any kind. Her Scottish upbringing and her life experiences did not leave her the choice to run or hide, so she knew she would stand her ground whatever the cost. She regretted bringing the two brothers into the middle of it but she also knew it was a decision they had made and not her.

Bartram and his ranch foreman pulled their horses up short of the three homesteaders, but did not dismount. August Bartram's face was red and his eyes narrowed down when he looked at Isla standing with a rifle in her hand. He did not remove his hat but spoke, directing his face and voice directly at Isla.

"Do you remember what I told you about not allowing my cattle access to the creek?"

"Do you remember what I told you about not trespassing on my property without permission?"

"I was told that you shot at my foreman." Bartram turned and pointed to the cowhand sitting off to his side.

"No, sir. That is not correct. I fired a warning shot, that's all. If I had been shooting at your foreman, he wouldn't be sitting on that horse."

"I'm not going to stand for you or these tenderfoot friends of yours intimidating my cowhands or my cattle."

"I'm not going to stand for you or your hands or your cattle trespassing on my land without permission."

"We'll see about that, Miss McNeese. Are you prepared to fight, because I'm not backing down? We'll be back and you better put that rifle up before you hurt someone or get hurt."

"You remember when we first met, I told you I came in peace and you treated me rudely? When you decide to act neighborly, I think we can work out an agreement. Until then, don't risk the lives of your cowhands or cattle by violating my property rights. And Mr. Bartram, you personally are not welcome on this homestead land."

Before Bartram could answer her, Frank Jamison spoke up. "That goes for our land too, Mr. Bartram. Trespassing is against the law. Come talk to us civil-like and let's see if we can't find a way to do this peacefully."

Bartram glared at Isla and then at Frank. "There is no law in these parts and I have more rifles than you do and I'm prepared to use them." On that challenge, the rancher turned his horse and called to his foreman, "Let's leave before I shoot one of these ...."

Frank looked at Isla, whose eyes were fixed on Bartram's backside. *She is a beautiful woman when her eyes look like that but I wouldn't want to cross her,* he thought to himself. *Maybe a change of subject is needed.*

"Isla, Alex is going to Cheyenne for more supplies and a wagon to haul them. Would you like to give him a list of things you need? We're buying produce and such but you might want something else and he can bring it back in the wagon if he can find a decent used one."

Isla blinked, she turned to Frank and almost smiled. "Thank you. I'll jot some things down. Just a minute."

The two brothers took the moment to discuss what had happened that morning and what their part in it might be.

"I hate bullies," Alex said.

"Me too, but I don't want to get killed. You need to look for a lawman while you are in town. Maybe the sheriff will help us settle this."

"You know I won't be back until tomorrow afternoon at best. Don't stand up to Bartram by yourself. Let it be. I need you safe, big brother."

"I can handle myself, but I don't intend to have a showdown on our property just yet. I'll wait for the law."

Isla came out the door with a piece of paper and a small roll of bills. She handed both articles to Alex and patted his wrist.

"You be careful, Alex. I've grown fond of you."

Alex blushed and said, "Yes, ma'am." He waved at his brother and broke his horse into a ground-eating jog.

Isla turned to Frank. "Thanks for coming back and warning me. Will I see you at lunch?"

Frank smiled, "Yes, ma'am. I'll bring some food."

"No, just some potatoes if you have them. I'm going fishing. Should be some nice trout in this stream and I aim to find out."

"You haven't fished in your own creek yet?"

"Been too busy. Besides, I want to be outside where I can watch things. I've got some corn for bait and there's always a hopper or two along the bank. Bring an appetite with the potatoes."

Frank tipped his hat and a grin spread across his face. "That's more like it, Isla."

FIVE

That same morning, Deloris had left the ranch with two cowhands and the ranch wagon for Cheyenne. Once a month she went into the city to shop for the ranch and herself. She stayed in the large new hotel and ate in the restaurant on the ground floor. The cowhands stayed somewhere, she wasn't sure where but they were never far away. If something happened to her, she was sure her dad would kill the hands or make them wish they were dead. Sometimes her dad went with her but not this time. He was too mad to even talk to.

She was several hours ahead of Alex, but the wagon was slower than Alex's horse since he was in a hurry and had a late start. Later, Deloris would reason that fate, chance, or the love goddess deemed it important that the two of them meet. Her first stop after the hotel was the Territory General Mercantile store. The store had started as a small building, but Cheyenne had grown so fast that the store had to enlarge. When Deloris arrived that evening, it was completing its third enlargement. It was amazing to the young Bartram to see all the different items now carried by the enterprise.

Deloris was shopping in the cloth and lace section when Alex walked in the door. She turned when he opened the door and immediately knew it was the young man who had moved next door to their ranch. It was obvious that he had not seen her because he had headed to another part of the store holding a list in his hand without staring at her. She expected staring. She decided to take her time in the lace department and see what would happen.

Alex kept carrying item after item to the front counter, stacking them together. Deloris began to give up hope of a chance meeting and decided that a more aggressive action needed to be taken. She was working on a plan when suddenly Alex showed up where the bolts of cloth were. He was looking at his list when his eyes saw her just over the edge of the paper. Deloris hid a grin when she saw him blush. Then she smiled ever so slightly and Alex blushed again. He didn't speak and she decided he couldn't speak and that made her feel funny. He was shy and that was unusual for young men in the west, but it pleased her somehow that he wasn't like the normal young men she had met on her trips to town.

She wasn't sure what the correct decorum was in the east but this was the frontier and decorum hadn't made it that far west. She walked around the counter and spoke.

"Aren't you the young man I saw with a hammer near Buffalo Creek recently?"

Alex face turned red and his lips moved but no sound came out. He nodded and tried to smile but it got mixed up somehow.

"My name is Deloris Bartram, what's yours?"

Alex struggled. He liked to talk; indeed, he did talk but suddenly he couldn't make words come out of his mouth.

"Cat got your tongue?"

"Al...Al...Alex. Alex Jamison."

"What are you men building?"

"Store. Store and stagecoach stop. I've got to go."

Alex put his list in his pocket and walked to the counter. He pointed to his collection of goods and said something to the clerk behind the sales counter and hastened out of the store. Deloris watched him leave and then allowed herself a complete smile. *He is different,* she said to herself.

Isla watched Frank ride off and then turned and headed for the house to clean up the morning dishes and to get some string and a hook to make good on her fish for lunch promise. Unaccountably, the edges of a smile played on the corners of her mouth.

Isla took off her boots and sat on the bank of the creek, allowing her feet to ease down in the water. "Yikes!" she said out loud and then laughed at herself. *I didn't think it would be this much colder than the air. In spite of the sun, the late summer air is pretty chilly.* She took a couple of pieces of the corn she had boiled and placed them on the hook. The water appeared clear but she knew she couldn't see as well as the trout.

She was anxious to learn what kind of trout were in Buffalo Creek. The land agent had said there were at least four species in the Territory. She told him that back in her home country of Scotland, the main trout was the brown. The agent told her that to find browns, she would have to go to the western end of the state. She really didn't care as she didn't know if one species tasted better than the other. She just wanted some trout. She should have thought of the fish earlier. If the stream held a good population, it would supplement hers and the Jamisons' table. The native trout would make a good item for the stagecoach restaurant menu as well.

She barely had time to think about it before the string was nearly jerked out of her hand. Slowly she played the fish and coiled the string between her legs. A ten-inch brook trout was attached to the small hook on her line. She admired the beautiful colors on the trout and placed it in a cloth sack and put the sack in the creek.

It soon became obvious that the creek held an abundant population of trout. None of her catches were much larger than the first small trout but she was pretty sure there were some larger ones in the creek behind the occasional rock. She quit fishing after the fifth trout. She didn't want to quit but she knew she had enough and she had lots of work to do. She also needed to think about August Bartram and her other neighbor, Ryan Gardener. *In fact, where was Ryan Gardener? I haven't seen him or his cattle so where is he watering them? I hope it's quite a distance upstream, beyond my viewing area. One confrontation a day was enough.*

Isla pulled her socks and boots back on and left the fish tied up in the bag in the shallow water. They would be nice and fresh when it came time to bake them for lunch. She ticked off the things she needed to do before fixing lunch. It was getting a little colder every day and that made her think of the root cellar. A few more feet and then she could line it with boards.

She wanted to add cheese to her milk by-products and it would do well in the cellar. Once it was finished, she would order some fruit and vegetables to store there.

She already felt the benefits of the work Frank had done on her walls. She knew it would really make a difference when the snow blew sideways off the distant mountains. She would ask him to do the same thing for the chicken coop. She probably should contract with Alex for a lean-to to provide shelter for Maggie at night and her during the milking. The land around her homestead was fairly flat and the winter wind could be a problem; blizzards were not uncommon, she had been told.

For some reason, she picked that moment to look over at the chickens. She studied them for some time and then said a word her mother had forbidden. Her favorite hen was missing.

Roy? Surely not or I would have seen the feathers. Same with a hawk or coyote. What then? One more thing to spoil my day just when I'm starting to rebound from my rude neighbor's visit. I need to work on the cellar and I can hen hunt after lunch is over. This day has already had as many adventures as I could possibly want.

She watched the sun as she used the pick and shovel, throwing the dirt onto a mound west of the cellar to form a wind break. She wanted time to bake the fish using some of her fresh butter and maybe make some fried bread. Her thoughts were interrupted by Roy's barking as he ran past her towards the lane and the front of the house. Isla dropped the shovel and picked up her rifle. She had been keeping it close at hand ever since Bartram's visit.

There were two riders coming up the lane from the stagecoach road. She recognized Carla and Ryan Gardener as soon as she saw them. Perhaps the mystery of where the Bar G's cattle had been the last few days was about to be explained. The couple sat their horses but Isla knew they wanted to go inside and talk. They had ridden too far just to say something from a horse's back. She hoped there was some coffee left. She could always make some more while they were making themselves comfortable but it would be nicer to start with a cup.

"Hello, neighbors," she called from the digging site, "light down and come in and visit. I love company and I could sure use a rest from that root cellar."

Carla gave Isla a smile as she dismounted, but Isla noticed that Ryan's face remained stern. Isla immediately noted that the couple was wearing working clothes so she knew it was not a social call to welcome her to the area. The two visitors followed her into the little house and she beckoned them to be seated at the small table.

"I assume you both drink coffee," Isla said.

"I'm not sure we'll be here that long, Miss McNeese. I have a business proposition I would like to talk to you about and it's going to be short and to the point. A take it or leave it proposition," Ryan answered.

"I'd like some coffee, Ryan. Just because we're here on business doesn't mean we can't be sociable and I need to rest after that punishing ride you led me on. We have the whole day for goodness's sake."

Isla turned to look in the morning's pot to hide her reaction to Carla's chiding of her husband. In her former marriage, talk like that would have resulted in her receiving a backhand across her cheek. She detected no such reaction from Ryan which was reassuring. She was pleased to find there was just enough of the brew left to fill three small cups. She filled them and sat them in the middle of the table and retrieved the small pitcher of cream from the morning's milking.

"Oh, Isla, you have a milking cow. When and where did you get her?" Carla asked and Isla knew it was sincere and not just small talk. She passed the cups and cream and sat down and related the story of the cattle, Roy, and Maggie.

"I'm a real cowgirl now and the fresh milk is so good. I've been sharing it with the Jamisons, you know, the two men who are opening a traveling post for the stagecoach. They are situated between my homestead and Mr. Bartram's ranch."

Ryan interrupted the milk story with the mention of his friend August. "That's one of the reasons we are here, Miss McNeese. A.B. just left us and I will tell you he is a very upset man and when he is upset, he can be dangerous."

"He wasn't always that way, Ryan," Carla said. "He just hasn't been the same since Eloise died. I worry about Deloris. It can't be good for her."

"Maybe not, but it is what it is. Did you shoot at Jake Meadows this morning Miss McNeese?" Ryan interjected.

"Did Mr. Bartram tell you I shot at his foreman?"

"Yes, he did. Are you denying it?"

"Obviously, he didn't listen to me when I explained what happened. Either that or he purposely told the story for the best effect and to make me look bad when he is the one who is to blame for this entire situation."

"Oh, really? Would you mind telling us what really happened? We would like to hear your version of the episode?"

"Sure, I've nothing to hide as he does. I told him I did not shoot at this Jake person or he would not be sitting on his horse. That's the fact. I'm a very good shot with a rifle and he was very close to me. Just across the creek actually. Had I intended to kill him, he would be dead. It's that simple."

"Hmm. What did A.B. do that you think he's trying to hide? Why are you blaming him for your actions?"

"I tried to be nice and neighborly to Mr. Bartram, but he was very rude to me. I told him not to cross my property line without asking permission. I felt we could work something out but he told me to leave and that he'd do what he wanted. His men brought their cattle to the creek right by where my cows are. I asked them to leave, but they refused; instead, they laughed at me. I fired a warning shot which scattered all the cows on both sides of the creek and the cowhands, too, I guess. Anyway, they left.

"When Mr. Bartram showed up a little later, I explained it to him again. He's of the opinion that my property line is of no consequence. He told me there was no law here and he would do what he wanted. Then he told Jake they should leave before he shot one of us. He used a very coarse word to describe us.

"Frank tried to reason with him too, but he wouldn't hear any of it. You can believe your friend but I'm going to tell you the same thing I told him; if you want to cross my land to water, then come and ask me and we'll see if we can work something out. I'm a single woman but I'm not scared; I've been through a lot in my life and worked hard since I was a little girl and I'm not going to be bullied off what is rightfully mine just because you have in his words, 'more rifles' than me. You may kill me but it will not be a cheap death and you will live with the knowledge that you wronged a woman who did you no wrong."

Carla looked at her husband. She was not smiling and her eyes were every bit as stern as his. "You're not like A.B., Ryan. Your wife is still alive, but I couldn't live with a man who mistreated a neighbor or took advantage of a woman."

Ryan did not respond immediately but held his coffee cup near his lips as if he was going to take a sip. He looked at Isla and then back at Carla. "You're right, dear. I'm not that kind of man. I told A.B. to back off, but he wouldn't listen. I want no part of this. I was upset at first, of course. But it's our fault. The creek has been there all the time and we could have bought the plot and split it in half and both had ample water. We didn't. Now we have to live with the consequences.

"Miss McNeese..."

Isla interrupted, "Please call me Isla. I want to be your neighbor and your friend."

"Well, all right. Isla, as I told you earlier, Carla and I came with a proposition that we think can solve this problem, at least our part of it. We would like to rent access to the creek at the western end of your property. It would be a little farther to the water but certainly not that much trouble. What would you consider a fair value?"

"How wide an access and would you want it fenced?"

"Maybe two hundred yards. We have a lot of cattle and we would take them to the creek in two or three different herds. No fences. The cowhands can keep them in the approved access."

"I like the idea. I want to be fair and I know how much cattle drink and I don't want them to suffer. I just want to be treated fair in return. Would you consider paying me in calves after calving time?"

"Yes, that is a terrific idea. Can we come to an agreement on how many?"

"I think since the price varies from year to year we should wait and talk about it after the spring calving. You'll be honest with me," Isla smiled, "and I know I can trust your lovely wife."

For the first time since meeting Ryan, Isla saw him smile, almost a grin.

"You got me there, Isla. It'll be as honest as my bookkeeping wife can make it."

"Then we have a deal. Let's all shake hands."

All three stood up and shook hands and the air seemed lighter and Isla knew she had done the right thing and so had the Gardeners. She expected the extra calves would help her grow a small herd faster than trying to buy them later in the year when they were yearlings. If only she could get Bartram to see that. Isla followed her guest out the door. When they were mounted up, Ryan looked at her.

"I think Carla and I will ride up to A.B.'s and make one more effort to calm him down. He was wrong and so was I. Maybe the two of us can help him see that. He'll listen to Carla better than me since she helped with his daughter, Deloris, when his wife died. "Thank you for your hospitality in a not-so-hospitable situation. We'll be in touch and the three of us will ride to the west end of the homestead and agree on the access placement."

Isla stood outside her door knowing she should be back at work on the cellar, but she wanted to treasure seeing the Gardeners turn north towards Bartram's. She took a minute to thank God for their change of heart and for their willingness to bring peace to the creek. *Blessed are the peacemakers,* she thought. *Am I being one? I hope so. I want peace and happiness. Everyone deserves some happiness, don't they?*

She gave the cellar a little more effort and then washed up to start lunch for her and Frank. She almost forgot Alex wouldn't be there. He was growing up and Frank was doing a good job as a father, mother and big brother. She thought again about the milking shed and shelter for Maggie. She had forgotten Balloch. It wouldn't do him any good to drift around in a snowstorm either.

She needed a small stable to house Balloch and Maggie and provide a milking stanchion. Frank and Alex wouldn't have time to get their own place ready with all the interference Bartram was creating, much less time for such a project as that would be. She didn't think she could do it by herself as every day the sun was rising later and setting earlier. She wasn't sure she could spare the time to go to Cheyenne and buy the lumber and hardware.

Frank was going to be a little late but she didn't mind as she was behind the sun herself. The trout were ready for the oven as soon as Frank brought the potatoes. She had mixed up the hoe cakes already and the batter was waiting for the flat surface of the wood stove. While she waited for Frank, she smoothed the coals under one of the metal eyes. She wanted an even fire for the cakes. She used all of her corn meal with the wheat flour and she wished she had added it to Alex's list. Once the potatoes were on the stove, she would cook the bread. *Hurry up, Frank!*

Frank and Isla sat down at the table, Isla's spread before them. For a moment, neither spoke, so glad were they to sit quietly and concentrate on being friends and without arguments or threats. It turned out that the hoe cakes were a big hit with Frank. He had eaten corn dodgers in the army but they weren't made the same way and were usually hard and greasy by the time they made it to the tin plates of the soldiers.

"These flat cornbread things are great. What do you call them?"

"In the Tidewater region where I lived, they were called hoecakes. I understand they were originally cooked over a wood fire on the blade of a hoe. Easy to make and very good. Batter has cornmeal and whole wheat flour with salt and a dab of sugar and a dollop of grease from the bacon drippings. I was told as part of my American history lessons that they were the favorite bread of George Washington. What about the fish? Do you like the brook trout?"

"Oh yes, it's just that the hoecakes are so different and tasty. Can I ask a question without you getting upset?"

"Of course, Frank. I'm okay now. Well, almost. What is the question?"

"Why did you leave the head and tail on the fish? Do Scottish people eat those?"

Isla couldn't hold back a short laugh. Her eyes lit up like Frank had not seen in a while.

"You know, Frank, I worked in a nice restaurant in Denver, and when people ordered trout from the menu, they wanted to be sure it was trout and not some cheap fish so the entire fish was served to show that it was a trout and what kind. We mostly sold rainbows because they are more plentiful in Colorado.

Maybe some people somewhere eat the head and tail but not in Denver or my Scotland.”

“Not to stir up bad memories, but I saw the Gardeners go up to Bartram’s and back down. Did they stop here? I wondered if Bartram told them about this morning’s altercation. It would be interesting to hear his side of the story.”

“As a matter of fact, they did stop by on their way up to Bartram’s. Actually, they didn’t decide to go see him until they talked to me. Ryan was told I shot at the foreman with intent to kill. I set the record straight. The Gardeners made me a business proposition. They will rent an access area at the west end of my property and pay me in calves next spring. What do you think of that?”

“Wow! That’s a big turnaround and sounds like a great idea. How many calves?”

“To be worked out based on market value. They were going to talk to Bartram and try to convince him to do the same thing on his side. He would have to give you something too I would think.”

“You think he’ll take the idea?”

“No, he’s hell-bent on having his way and he isn’t going to give in to a woman. I’m going to leave it alone tomorrow with Alex gone, but I will go have a word with him about respecting my rights. You’re welcome to accompany me.”

“I sure don’t like the idea of you going alone. I’m not saying that to lessen your ability to handle the man, but I think there should be a witness to what he says and what he does. If it's okay, I would like to go. When do you plan on going?"

"I'll wait until Jake, the foreman, goes back and reports that nothing happened. That will make Bartram think he's won. Might put him in a better mood for talking things over. I'm saying might. I don't like the man, to be honest."

"Me neither. He talked down to Alex and I like he was some cattle baron or king of the range and we were opportunists and didn't care about the land or the cattle business. Really a difficult man to talk to. I had to nudge Alex twice to keep him from speaking up. The boy doesn't seem so bashful around August Bartram."

"Okay, I'll stop by on my way up, say an hour or so after the cattle leave. I'm going to be busy this afternoon looking for a lost hen and trying to finish that root cellar. The days are really getting shorter. Winter's coming soon, I'm afraid. By the way, thanks for the caulking you did, the cabin is much warmer now. Which made me think that I might need a place for Maggie so I can easily milk her when the rough weather comes. Think Alex could help with that?"

"I don't see how, Isla. We're behind ourselves and we need a tight storefront and rear quarters for us and a place for our horses and the chickens you're going to sell us. This mess with the ranchers has interrupted our work too many times. And of course, we have to come visit you. Time well spent, mind you."

"What am I going to do, Frank, I can't take care of livestock, fix meals for three people and keep house and build a stable or barn."

"Hmm, problem alright. Unless we get some clear nights with a bright moon, the time is going to get less every day. Plus, you will have to make a trip to Cheyenne for materials and that will take two full days. If Alex gets a wagon and draw horse you can use it to get the things you need."

"Oh, I guess I'll just have to do the best I can. Lunches may not be so grand for a few weeks."

"Don't worry about it. We'll help all we can, you know that. Say, didn't you tell me once that an older gentleman helped you build this cabin and put the iron stove together? Henhouse too, right? Is he available?"

Isla looked dumbfounded, and then she frowned and then smiled.

"Of course, how stupid of me. I offended him somewhat by telling him I could finish the house myself. He wanted to work. Said he liked working for me. Wonder if he's still upset with me. If he's not too busy in the city, he just might come up and help us both. When I go get the materials, I will look him up and offer him the job. Where will he sleep, I wonder? Getting too cold to sleep outside under a wagon, I imagine."

"That sounds like a great plan, I bet you feel better already. Now, I'll help clean up lunch and get back to work on the *Jamison Stagecoach Stop-By*."

"Is that what you're going to call it?"

"I don't know, that just popped out because I'm in a good mood all of a sudden."

"You go to work on the *Jamison Stagecoach Stop-By* and I'll take care of the *Isla Eatery*."

They both laughed and Frank went out the door, humming as he put his work hat on.

SIX

Cleaning up was the easiest thing in the world that afternoon and there was fish, potatoes and hoecakes enough for supper. She could work right up to Frank's arrival. If she could find her missing hen or evidence of her demise quickly, she could finish digging the cellar. She was several feet under the earthen roof now. She wanted it to be about ten feet by ten square. Next year she would have garden things to put away for the winter.

She hung her apron up, grabbed her rifle and headed for the rear of the house. It was actually a cabin but she thought of it as a house, her house. She walked past the hen house, counting her hens. The red and light brown hen was still missing. *Maybe she should call Roy to help but she was afraid it might confuse him and she didn't know how to direct him to find a red and brown missing hen.*

She walked past the cellar site and turned due west towards some low brush growing almost out of sight.

Maybe the hen was hiding in the rough cover. She might have a nest hidden under one of the low-lying shrub-type plants. Not too wise, perhaps, but still possible.

Just as she neared the brushy area, the mother hen came strutting out of the underbrush, clucking her head off. Right behind her came eight fluffy yellow and brown chicks running for all their worth, trying to keep up with the one in front and their clucking momma. Isla gave a sigh of relief.

"Ah ha, missy. Looks like you have some chicks that can go to the Jamisons in a few weeks. Aren't you the sly one? I've been so stressed I haven't kept track of you girls like I should have. We better get you in the hen house and shut the door. I saw a Cooper's Hawk this morning circling around the creek. You know they're bird eaters and these babies are definitely birds. Come along, chicks. Come on chick, here chicks, chicks."

Isla found herself humming as she chopped and dug. Frank was having an effect on her. She almost blushed. Well, she guessed he was. She was tired of eating alone and he was obviously a nice man who made no advances. *Was that because he is nice,* she wondered *or because he doesn't find big ole me attractive? Anyway, things would be so good if neighbor August would change his attitude.*

Sure enough, she finished the digging before dark. She went to the house and got her milking things and started her search for Maggie. She called for Roy, and in a minute, she saw the cow coming over the small rise followed closely by the little cattle dog snapping at her heels. *That is one smart dog. I'm so lucky to have him."*

She closed the stanchion around Maggie's neck and sent Roy off to take care of his charges.

"Thank you, Roy, I'll have some left-over scraps for you tonight that I'm sure you'll like."

When her bucket was filled, she turned Maggie loose and took the milk to the cellar and covered it with a cloth It would sit overnight in the coolness of the cellar and she would separate the cream in the morning. More butter was going to be needed for biscuits. She also was planning on pancakes when Alex got back with the supplies she had ordered.

When she left the cellar, there was still some light so she decided to walk to where the cows were and see how they were faring. She often thought of pinching herself to see if she was dreaming or just living a real-life dream. The cows were bunched up for the night and Roy was lying on the ground a few feet away. He got up when he heard her coming and came over to her.

She was embarrassed that she had spent such little time with him. She grabbed his head and scratched between his ears. He too, wanted attention and did his best to get as close to her as he could. It was surprising to her because she thought of him as a working dog, not a companion. She had spent almost no personal time with him, but it was obvious that in the past, he had been someone's best friend. She made a promise to him that she would do better. Maybe he could come in before lunch for a few minutes each day. The cows would be resting from the morning eating and drinking and his work would be light at that time. He needed her, she reasoned, and she definitely needed him.

Roy raised up and growled, then barked. He shot off for the house and she knew that Frank was coming up the trail from the road. Roy seemed to like Frank, too, but it didn't prevent him from announcing the arrival of guests. She stood up straight and quicken her steps. Supper would be ready in a jiffy but she wanted to tell Frank about the baby chicks and hear what he did in the afternoon. *If only her first marriage had been with a friend like this. Did she think the word first? Was she thinking of a second marriage? Slow down, Isla, slow down. You just met the man."*

They met at the door and both started talking at the same time, each happy to see the other and eager to share. "You first, Isla. Did you find your lost layer?"

"Yes, I did. She was in the brush in the back and guess what? She has eight little chicks. In a few weeks, I'll be able to give you two men some chickens, one or two of all ages. Isn't that exciting? Oh, I finished digging the cellar so now all it needs is something to line it with and a door. Goodness, what a chore that has been. We have fresh milk for breakfast and hopefully some fresh butter. Fresh milk, butter and eggs. All we need is a hog. No, forget that. I'll buy the bacon; I don't want to mess with a hog. Too much work and all of it dirty. Come on in and tell me about your afternoon while I get the food warmed up. I hope Alex is all right."

As it turned out, Alex was doing better than all right. After leaving the general store, he went to the horse and mule sale barn in search of a wagon and a draft-type horse. Maybe a stout Morgan that could also pull a plow for a garden. He found exactly what he wanted. Someone had traded in an older model buckboard that had been used to haul light freight. Buckboards normally had seven-inch side boards but these were twice that height, probably nearer to eighteen inches. It was in good shape; the axles were greased and recently, the wheels had new iron bands wrapped and shrunk on the solid hickory.

The body, seat and buckboard were also hickory. It was a good thing because the buckboard looked like it had been kicked a few times. Several nicks and one dent were evidence of the board's value. The lengthy springboards that made up the eight by three-foot bed were also solid-aged hickory and seemed springy enough to give a decent ride. The wagon had never been painted so it was probably privately owned. The price was reasonable and the dealer threw in a set of harnesses. Not new, but serviceable.

"Ever drive one of these rigs, son?"

"No, sir. Not a buckboard."

"Well, you steer it with the front wheels. The axle pivots as you turn. Easy to make short turns. You'll like it for light duty. Invented by a doctor, I heerd. 'Bout fifty years ago. Depending on where they're built, they have different woods. This one was probably made in the Tennessee area 'cause the whole thing is nice seasoned hickory."

Next, he took Alex to look over the horses and sure enough, Alex spotted a nice-looking mare that appeared to be part Morgan. Back in the late 1700s, a bay horse was sold to a schoolmaster named Justin Morgan. Horses were known by their owner's name and so Figure, his real name, was known in the town as the Justin Morgan Horse. Justin bred the stallion and that started the famous Morgan breed though he did not live long enough to get the credit. Known for smarts and loyalty, they were hard workers for their size. It was said that Figure could out trot, outrun and outwork any horse in town. Just what he and Frank had in mind. He had to dicker a little, but he and the dealer soon agreed on a reasonable price that satisfied both. *A good way to make a trade*, Alex thought.

The dealer helped him hook the dark-colored horse up and showed him how the old harness worked.

"The mare is about ten years old," the dealer said, "but in good shape. She has been well taken care of by someone who knows horses. It was an ex-railroad employee who got hurt but was able to keep one of his horses. He fell on hard times recently and had to sell the horse. He told me that the mare's name is Maude.

"Interesting name for a horse, don't you think?" the dealer asked.

"I guess I can handle it," Alex responded with a slight grin. He knew he wasn't much of a talker and he wanted to get on with his business anyway.

The dealer agreed to let Alex go load his merchandise and bring the horse and wagon back for the night. "I'm up early and I don't guess it'll hurt to feed the old girl one more night. You paying in hard money or paper?"

"I got some of both."

"Well, that paper money's only been around for ten or so years and even if it says legal tender on it, I still like cold hard cash. But to stay in business, you got to do what you got to do."

The two of them went into the makeshift office and the dealer wrote out a bill of sale for the Morgan, wagon and harness. Alex counted out the money and the two of them shook hands. Alex tied his horse to the rear of the wagon and set Maude in motion. He laughed as he thought of the horse's name. *Seemed more appropriate for a mule than a workhorse. Maybe the former owner knew something about the horse that he didn't. He guessed he would find out.*

Once the wagon was loaded and the rig was returned to the paddock of the horse and mule barn, Alex headed for the Plains Hotel on the corner of 16th and Plains. He planned on staying the night there and eating supper. He had eaten a plain sandwich Isla had hastily made for lunch and in spite of the healthy breakfast Isla had fed him, he was feeling pretty hungry. He turned his horse over to the hotel stable hand and went in to sign up for a room and find a table.

He stepped into the large dining room and paused to look for an empty table. He was surprised to hear his name called from the left side of the room. Then his face failed him once again as he saw Deloris Bartram waving him over. More talk? She was at a table for four but she was alone.

"Well, Mr. Jamison, I see we meet again. Please join me as I hate to eat alone in such a large dining room with so many strangers and me a poor defenseless girl."

Alex took the chair opposite hers and nodded. He finally was able to speak but it was an effort. "I don't hardly see you as a poor defenseless girl, Miss Bartram."

She gave him one of her best smiles. "Well, I needed a reason to ask you to join me since we are almost strangers even though we live just a mile or so apart. My name is Deloris and yours is Alex, right? Can we drop the mister and miss last name business? We're neighbors and I hope we can be friends since we do live next door."

"Yes, that's fine. I mean first names are fine but I'm not sure we can be much in the way of friends even though we are neighbors. My brother and I have not gotten off on a good footing with Mr. Bartram. I think he hates us but I'm not really sure why."

"Pooh, he'll come around, you'll see. He's carrying a big burden and can't put it down. It makes him cross and unsociable. I'll have a little talk with him. We're good friends, as well as daughter and father. Now let's find out about you. Oh, here comes the waiter. What do you want, do you know?"

"I'll have to look at the bill of fare. I've never been here and I'm not rich so I better wait and see what they have and how much it costs before I decide."

"Well, it's not real cheap but not too high and everything is good. Dad and I eat here every month when we come to shop for the ranch."

The waiter walked up to the table and addressed Deloris. "Has madam ordered yet?"

"No, I've not. Give us a few minutes to look over the list. I'll have lemonade to drink, please."

"And you, sir?"

"Do you have sassafras tea?"

"The highest quality, sir. Would a pint be sufficient?"

"That would be fine, thank you."

The waiter left and while Alex looked over the printed card, Deloris used the opportunity to learn more about her new friend.

"I see that you can talk when it's important to you, friend Alex. I guess food is important to a young man. How do you feel about young ladies?"

Alex looked up from the bill of fare and blushed, although not as bad as the first one. He gave her question some thought and answered slowly to control his runaway emotions.

"I've had a lot more experience with food than young ladies, Deloris. I think after meeting you, I may endorse young ladies. Is that a satisfactory answer?"

It was not at all what she had expected and his straightforward answer told her a lot about young Alex. To be truthful, at the age of seventeen and living twenty-five miles from Cheyenne, she had little experience with young men, but she had lived the last few years as the only female around a ranch flowing over with young and old men. Perhaps being around the cowboys led her to think she would like to know if all young men were the same. Alex appeared to lack such curiosity about ladies.

She already knew she liked Alex, and she felt bad that he had perhaps been mistreated by her father. She wanted to know more about him and why he was as he was and why he was with his brother and not a family. It wasn't really romantic, she told herself, but then it might be. She never had a romantic encounter and wasn't too sure what that entailed anyway. She knew it wasn't like her relationship with her father or Jake or one of the younger ranch hands, but what was it exactly? She knew just sitting and talking to Alex was a new and exciting experience.

Their food soon came and while Alex mostly chewed and drank his sassafras tea, he did pause long enough to give Deloris answers to her questions. Not long answers but answers. *Obviously, Deloris thought, Alex did not grow up where there was lots of chatter at the table. Probably he and his brother paused from working for a quick bite and were too tired to talk.* She would have been surprised at how little Alex talked at the table before he started eating with Isla.

His sudden interest in Deloris was drawing the real Alex out of his hiding place.

When the meal was over, Deloris made one final attempt at getting to know Alex better and hopefully for him to know her better. *How could a friendship develop if you didn't spend time together and talk? They were neighbors so they should be friends, and she already knew she was going to like him as a friend.*

"Alex, when are you starting back to Buffalo Creek?"

"Early."

"Well, how early?"

"I don't know, sunup, I guess."

"That early?"

"I have to work, Deloris, and my brother is doing my share as well as his. The wagon is loaded down and will be slow. So yes, dawn at the latest."

"What about breakfast?"

"It'll have to wait. I can't."

Deloris showed her first frown or perhaps just frustration that her plan was not going to work out.

"I was hoping we could travel together and visit on the long journey. I could ride with you or you with me and one of the cowhands could drive the other wagon."

"Get up before dawn and be ready to go."

"I have to eat."

"You won't die. Order some food and take it with you. You can pretend it's a picnic as you let someone else drive."

Was he stubborn or just that dedicated? What did it say about his feelings for their new friendship? No, better not go there. You caught him by surprise and this is all your doing, not his. He didn't take part in the planning. Your choice, Miss Smarty Pants.

"Okay, you win. I'll have my wagon and guys ready at daybreak. I'll order food for the entire party and we can eat, travel and talk together."

SEVEN

When Frank had left the property, Isla took a large pail out to the creek and brought water back, which she placed on the still hot stove. She undressed and did her nightly cleansing. The water was dark when she tossed it out the door later. The root cellar work had left her dirtier than usual and the warm water felt good. After the morning's events, she had felt dirty even before tackling the cellar. She brushed her hair with extra strokes and put on her nightgown. She was so tired she fell asleep on the way down to her pillow.

It wasn't just the warm bath or the good supper that relaxed her, it was knowing that she would not react negatively the next morning but go about her business as if everything was all right. To make sure, she promised herself that she would not go outside armed to the teeth. She would wave if she saw the cowhands and that would be it. No matter what they said or did.

The next dawn found the entire neighborhood up and at work. On the creek, Isla was taking care of the milking and the previous night's milk. Frank was getting as much work on the store done as possible before joining Isla for their morning breakfast. The hands at the Rocking AB were already eating in preparation for moving the cattle to water and a different grazing area.

In the growing and bustling city of Cheyenne, two wagons loaded with various merchandise were headed for the Fort Laramie stagecoach road and miles north. One wagon was driven by a ranch hand, as its regular driver was seated next to Alex Jamison, who was driving his own newly purchased conveyance. The conversation began before the group reached the main street leading out of town. It would be a long trip. In addition, one of the Mexican cowboys had bought a used guitar the night before and had wrapped his reins around the large Mexican roping post on his saddle and was attempting a Mexican love song. In honor of his boss's daughter, of course. Yes, it would be a long day.

On the creek, Isla felt good about her early start, she had quickened the milking time, recovering skills she had not used in a long time. It was still in her muscle memory, though, and Maggie was getting better. Roy had the system figured out and as soon as he heard the door close, he hunted up Maggie and started her to the stanchion. A shed would speed it up even more, holding her in at night.

She would be glad when Alex got back with the supplies as breakfast would be buttered two-day-old bread from off the stove top, fresh milk, fresh cream and coffee and very fresh eggs. Considering the circumstances, they should feel blessed, she knew that. For some reason, she felt better up and working than before she went to bed the previous night. If life could just go on like this, she could eat eggs and drink milk every day.

Isla backed out of the cellar with the previous night's milk and was startled by Roy's barking. He had not heard the message that the cowhands and cattle were to be ignored that day. She stopped and shaded her eyes from the just-rising rays of bright light. It was a large group of cows to bring at one time and there were additional drovers as well. She did not move until they were spread along the bank and in the creek. Fortunately, none tried to venture across, mostly because a barking dog waited on the opposite bank. When things settled down, she started toward the house, making a closer creek approach than was necessary.

She noticed that all the men near the creek were holding their carbines in their hands and pointed to the sky. She turned and waved and walked purposely to her front door without looking back. She wanted to look back, of course, and she wanted to see the surprise on their faces, but looking back would have spoiled it, at least for her. Roy, on the other hand, had no such limitations. He moved up and down the creek bank, watching the other side of the stream and giving an occasional bark if a cow came too close.

Everything sat on the table except the coffee and Isla was pouring it when Frank knocked on the door. She yelled at him to come in and make himself useful and he entered grinning at her cheerful voice.

"I see the Rocking AB is out early and in full force. Loaded for bear and itching for a fight, I wouldn't wonder," he said as he rang up his hat.

"Oh, yes. Guns to intimidate a helpless woman. I just waved and turned my back as if I didn't have a care in the world. Wish I could have seen their faces. Bet their noses fell to their chins. Roy had no qualms about making his opinion heard, though. He's keeping them at bay. I hope Alex is getting an early start. I sure would like some bacon to go with these good eggs, potatoes too." *Oh, Isla, what did you say about eating fresh eggs and milk in exchange for this good life?*

Frank offered to say grace and she was pleased. He mentioned his brother and that pleased her more. It felt like family. *Watch it, Isla.*

"Did you get much done this morning, Frank?"

"Up before the sun and got a full day's work organized. Weather looks good, so I should get a lot done. I may just make a snack and stay at the store rather than lose the hour to come and eat. Just for today. Alex would never stand for that: 'Not eat with Miss Isla? No, no.'"

Isla laughed. "I think I'd say no, no, too. Having friends to eat with is certainly habit forming and it's nice to share the good and the bad, don't you think?"

"I didn't say I didn't want to come..."

"I know, at least I think I know how you feel. It can be a lonely place out here in the wide-open spaces and most humans don't like loneliness."

"Might be what's bothering Bartram, Isla."

"He's not alone, he's got his daughter and his cattle."

"Not the same though, is it?"

She looked at him for several seconds. She knew what he was saying and no, it wasn't the same as having a partner.

"You're right, of course, but he still scares me."

"Yes, it is a tricky situation and it could get worse. What you are doing today may settle the pot. I saw worse things in the war. I mean selfishness, inhumanity, anger and greed. I understood Noah's ark better after my second major battle. Some men crying and some men laughing, sadness and gladness at the pain of others. We should try to avoid harming each other as best we can. Doesn't the Good Book say something about living at peace with all men?"

"It does. As much as lies in you. I'm just not sure how much lies in me. You don't know what it feels like to be treated so offhandedly because you are the so-called weaker sex. I don't want war; I want peace, and a little happiness thrown in wouldn't hurt."

"It's what we all want, I think, but sometimes things get mixed up and prevent us from seeking it like the Constitution says we have the right to. Not the happiness but the pursuit of it."

"You surprise me, Frank. I didn't realize you were a man of letters."

"I went two years to a military academy before the war. Why I wound up in the war in the first place, I guess. It was expected, no, nearly demanded."

"What was your favorite thing to study?"

"Literature, especially poetry and essays. No monetary future in it but a comfort when working hard at other things or fighting a war against your own people. Are you familiar with Elizabeth Barrett Browning?"

"We had schools in Scotland and the Scottish people can read and many, many of us love the English poets. I personally find them much more interesting than the American poets. The American poets seem stiffer, more practical, and less sensitive, especially in their romantic works. Just my opinion."

"Well, this is something new. I have an idea. Why don't the three of us take turns at breakfast one morning a week reciting a favorite work? Alex is learning to love literature as well. He missed it growing up with foster parents."

"I love the idea. Let's do it on Mondays and start our work week out positive."

"I don't know about you, but I don't seem to have a non-work day at the *Jamison Stagecoach Stop-By*."

"You know what I mean, Frank. On Sunday, we can read the scriptures and pray. Would you like that? I sense you're a believer."

"War secured that for me. Maybe not that there is a God, but that a God is essential if mankind is to have any hope. Are you a Catholic, Isla?"

"No, I'm Scottish Presbyterian, or at least that's how I was raised. We better get to work; this is getting to be too much fun and you especially have a lot to do. I wish I could come help, but I need to keep moving too."

"When do you want to visit the Rocking AB?"

"After supper, but before dark. Can you come just a little early? There's not much to eat anyway. If I have time, I might take Roy out to the brushy area and see if we can scare up a rabbit or something."

"Sure, say an hour earlier. That'll give us time to get there without seeming in a hurry. Alex may make it home by then."

"I don't want him in on this. He'll be tired but he can unload the light stuff while we make our case for peace and, of course, the pursuit of happiness."

The afternoon moved quickly for Isla as she bustled from task to task. She started with dusting the few things hanging on the wall of the main room. There was a small portrait of her parents made when she was a young girl in the highlands; a painting of Jesus she had purchased from a traveling artist in Denver; and, an embroidered piece of colorful heathers her mother had made before she left home. It wasn't much but it brought her great comfort when the lonelys hit her.

She found a couple of cobwebs in the furthest corners but decided to leave them for the time being because you never knew when you might need to staunch a blood flow. All the kitchenware got a good scrubbing, including the stove. She removed the ashes and carried them outside and sprinkled them in a dying flower bed. *In the spring, they would make a difference,* she thought. She so wanted beautiful flowers around the front door. Her mother always had fresh flowers.

The table and chairs got a good going over and then she tackled the floor. Not just a good sweep, but a real scouring with an old stiff brush she had packed away for just such a use. Due to her happy heart, the tasks whisked by and before the milking time loomed near, she picked up her rifle and went in search of Roy and possible meat for supper. *Like the old pioneers,* she thought.

Roy managed to send two yearling rabbits past her and she dispatched them both on the run. Taking a piece of string out of her pocket, she tied their feet together and threw them over her shoulder. In minutes she had them skinned, gutted and washed in fresh creek water. *I'll see if there's an old onion left in a nook or cranny or maybe some wild herbs near the creek. Anyway, we aren't going hungry.*

Isla moved slowly down the edge of the creek, hoping to spot an onion or leek that had been delayed by the cold spring and late summer. In cold climates, she knew that sometimes they would still be growing when the next winter was just starting out. A quarter of a mile up the creek, way past where she normally walked, she found a small patch of wild onions. The six petal yellow flowers were gone but when she pulled a few plants up, the onions were developed and full of strong odor. They were still strong enough that she only needed a small handful of the smallest ones. Now her smile became a grin. *Wouldn't Frank be surprised?*

The acknowledgment that that fact mattered stopped her in her tracks. She looked across the creek in the direction of the occasional hammering sound. *So be it,* she whispered to herself. It also made her pleased that she could make a surprise for someone.

Frank whistled when he opened the door and the rabbit meat and wild onion mess wafted past his nose. "What do we have, Miss McNeese? Do I smell rabbit and onions?"

"Yes, you do. I shot two and found a small patch of late onions. The coffee is gone but the milk has been in the cellar all day and it's cool out there anyway. Hot rabbit and cold milk. That's supper, but it'll be filling and will make us feel good on the way over."

Midway through the oohs and ahhs of the supper, their interesting conversation was interrupted by Roy who came by the cabin at full bark. Frank jumped up and cracked the door open.

"It's Alex and he's got a fine horse and buckboard and the wagon's piled up pretty good. I'll tell him to wash in the creek and come eat while it's still hot. I guess we left him some. He can unload your stuff when we leave, and then I'll unload at our place when we come back."

Alex came in the door and both Frank and Isla sensed that something wasn't just right. He hugged them both, but then sat down and took the plate Isla handed him without much enthusiasm. They expected an outburst of information about the trip and the shopping experience. Frank, of course, had questions about the wagon and horse and the prices of their merchandise.

Alex looked at them both, the fork filled with rabbit near his mouth. "I don't want to talk, please. Maybe later. I've heard all the talk I want to hear for today and tomorrow too."

"What happened?" the two adults asked in unison.

"Please! Later, tomorrow or the next."

"You sure don't talk much," Frank said.

"I've heard that sentiment enough for one day, thank you."

Frank and Isla shook their heads and sat down and finished their half-eaten supper. Between bites, Frank shared his plan with Alex but did not ask for input. All he said when he finished was, "That okay with you?"

Alex shook his head. Murmured how good the food and milk were and continued eating, his mind seemingly in some other place. Frank and Isla were still pondering where it might be when it was time to leave.

"I'll clean up when I get back, Alex. Just unload my things and go home and rest in well-earned solitude."

EIGHT

The two of them spent so much time talking about how strange Alex seemed after such an adventure that they almost forgot to discuss their strategy for their looming meeting with rancher Bartram.

They arrived just in time to see the last of the ranch's household goods being carried inside by some of the ranch hands. August Bartram and his teenage daughter sat side by side in whitewashed rockers just down the porch from the door. August appeared to be getting a running account of the two-day shopping trip he had failed to make. He was suddenly wishing that he had yielded to her and traveled in spite of the ranch business of the last few days.

The two of them stood up as Isla and Frank dismounted and tied their horses to the rail. Deloris pushed by her father and ran towards Isla.

"You must be the famous Isla I've heard so much about. You're the tallest woman I've ever seen and my dad described you just right. He just forgot to mention how attractive you are. My name is Deloris. You must be Alex's brother, Frank. He's told me so much about the two of you. I'm so excited. I had no idea you would be coming over with all that merchandise to unload and so much excitement to hear about. Did you come to see me or father?"

Isla took advantage of the question to get a word in. Even as she did so, a picture describing Alex's odd behavior began to form in her mind.

"No, Miss Deloris. We came to speak to Mr. Bartram about our sharing the creek in a sane and peaceful way. Do you suppose we could have a few minutes with him and then I'd love to hear whatever it is you are all heightened up about?"

Deloris gave a pretense of blushing and then apologized. "I'll just go clean up while you adults talk. Nice to meet you both."

She stopped and said something to her father as she walked by him on the edge of the steps where he had moved after her rush to the yard. He frowned, shook his head and motioned her to go on inside.

"You people come up on the porch. I'll get us another chair. I hope this is not going to be a lengthy conversation because I've had a long day and I haven't eaten yet and I've got to be up early. Besides, we already talked about this whole thing and your mind is made up and so is mine. Since things went so well today, I'll give you a short hearing. Have a seat."

Isla took the farthest seat, putting Frank between her and where she thought August would put his chair. She was trying to calm her thoughts and get complete control of her emotions. She knew she was right, but she couldn't ignore the feeling that rancher Bartram might not care about right or wrong. She prayed for inner peace and for Frank that he would not feel a need to do or say something unnecessary to protect their budding friendship. That's all she would call it.

August came back out the door carrying a dining room chair and set it down almost equal distance from the two of them.

"Okay, let's get it over with. I'm listening but I'm not going to argue into the night. State your case and I'll state mine; then I want you off my ranch and I want you to stay off. I'll post an armed guard if need be."

Isla did not speak for a few moments but studied her adversary closely. She wanted complete control of her words and her demeanor. She leaned forward, placing her weight on her arms, and resting pointedly on the side of the rocker.

"That's interesting, the way you put that, Mr. Bartram. You think you have a right to refuse entrance to your property, but at the same time, you believe you have the right to cross into ours anytime you feel the urge. How does that rank in fairness to you?" Isla asked.

"I was here long before you two showed up with your little dreams. What am I supposed to do, just give up my big dreams for your privacy? I'm running one of the largest ranches in the southern part of the Wyoming Territory and I'm running it successfully. You come along and threaten to ruin twenty-five years of hard work I put in before moving here. It's not going to happen, you hear me?"

"We are not ruining twenty-five years or one year. We have no intentions of ruining your plans for your ranch, yourself or your daughter. We are asking to be treated with fairness and decency, two things you have neglected to do. Things you were once good at, I've been told. Are you aware of the deal Ryan and Carla Gardener made with me?"

"Yes, the backstabbers told me all about it. I'm not going to give you free calves for water and grass that

I've been freely using for the past several years. It certainly isn't my job to subsidize your personal enterprises."

"Frank and I didn't own our homesteads so many years ago, just a few days, as you know. But the legal fact is that we own them now and you are violating Territorial laws in addition to God's law of treating your brother as yourself. We don't want to call in the law or to cause undue trouble for you or your daughter. Let's just do what is fair and be friends."

"Miss McNeese, Frank, I'm not going to coddle either of you. I'm moving my cattle to Buffalo Creek every day in the foreseeable future and you had better stay out of the way or you might have a nasty accident. Accidents happen in the wild west you know. I've offered you more than a fair profit on your venture and your stubbornness is going to cost you. The Rocking AB will thrive and you will disappear in the winter storms. Life will go on to the strongest as it should. And by the way, I have no interest in being friends or being friendly with any of you."

Isla stood up, hair on the back of her neck rising along with red blood in her Scottish face. Peaceful people, but don't put their backs against the wall. All things fight when trapped and threatened. She did a rare thing. She stepped up close to her adversary and put her index finger a few inches from his nose.

"Carla told me about your wife. Not just about her sudden departure but her manner of life while she was here. If she can see and hear you tonight up in heaven, she must be the first person to ever shed tears in paradise. If you persist in this course of action, I feel certain you will never see her again, nor should God allow it. Good night, Mr. Bartram and one more time, in your own words: I want you off my ranch and I want you to stay off or you and your cowboys might have a wild west accident. They happen here, I'm told. I'm leaving, Frank, you can stay and try to reason with an unreasonable man if you want."

August did not speak and during the ensuing silence, Frank stood up and joined Isla. "I've had enough of ignorance for one night, thank you. Let's go home and clean our weapons."

The visitors reached their mounts just as the front door of the house opened with a bang. Deloris reached her father and hit him in the chest with both fists.

"How dare you shame my mother's memory with such behavior. Have you no respect for the dead? And how about the living? I will not live in the same house as a thief and murderer. Do not come near me, I mean it."

Tears running down her face and sobs shaking her body, she fled back inside the door, pulling it closed with such force it shook in its solid fir frame. It was obvious that August was in shock, but neither Frank nor Isla felt sorry for him. They were struggling to mount up and leave, fighting to control their thoughts and behavior. Both were concerned for Deloris. How far would a man as twisted as August Bartram go?

Frank made an unheard threat and promise. Isla was somewhat more vocal. Once on the road, the trip to their homesteads was made in somber silence. Unknown to them, the incident had pushed them closer together than the circumstances seemed.

Isla was so emotionally upset that she skipped her nightly toilet routine. Her boots hit the floor and her outer jacket fell over the small straight-back chair beside the old feather bed. She blew out the candle on the bedside table and her body hit the mattress simultaneously with her head. She rolled on her back and stared in the dark at the wooden underside of the roof. Her heart cried out to God; sleep was long and hard in the getting.

At the Jamisons', Frank related to Alex what Bartram said but kept his words as calm as possible. He did not ask Alex any questions about his ride home with the Deloris girl. Under the circumstances, it seemed an inappropriate thing to do and Alex obviously didn't want to talk about it. Frank hoped the night's events didn't complicate whatever happened on the trip from Cheyenne.

"Tomorrow is probably not going to be a good day. I think we better be up early. Let's get this stuff put away and get to bed. We might want to clean our weapons and have them handy. I don't know what to expect exactly since we're not the major object of the action but I don't think it's going to be good."

Dawn came at the expected moment in time and it found the Buffalo Creek occupants up and busy as normal. Emotions were everywhere on the emotional map with everyone except Roy. Roy was just up and doing his job the best he knew how. He had no clue he was about to be in a storm and it's just as well since he would be free to act spontaneously. He was aware that Maggie was called almost an hour earlier than usual and that his mistress was unduly quiet and somber. She had gone back into the house and stayed. He kept looking for the two men who came every morning, but they did not show up.

It was then that Roy heard the sound of the cattle and their drivers. The sound was unusual. Louder than before and there was yelling and gunfire. He pushed his charges away from the creek bank and moved to the edge of the water to see what was happening. He heard the front door open and saw Isla step into the yard and walk to the creek bank. She was carrying the stick that killed the rabbits. He wasn't sure if he should go to her or stay with the cattle. The cattle were his job but she was his boss and he was rapidly falling in love with her.

Isla walked tall and steady to the creek bank and watched the cows coming in a rush to the creek. So heavy was the stream of cattle that the ones in front were pushed across the water. When the first steer hit her side of the creek, she put a 30-30 bullet through its head. Then the second and the third. She kept firing until the old rifle was empty. Quickly, she pulled shells out of her jacket and stuffed them into the receiver and fired again. The cows were confused. They tried to turn away from the carnage and began to fall into the water, trampling and being trampled. It was colossal chaos and a huge mess.

Across the creek, more confusion issued as the cowhands tried to stop what they had started. Two hands fell off as solid steers rammed into their horses. There was yelling and screaming. Coming up from the stagecoach road and riding hard was August Bartram. He held his rifle up by his head and was yelling at the top of his lungs. It was unclear whether he was yelling at the milling cattle, the cowhands or the entire scene in general.

Isla swung to her right and pointed her rifle toward the charging rancher. The rifle spoke once and once only. It completely changed the charged atmosphere for every human being who witnessed the result. Bartram's horse stumbled and then crumpled to the ground. Bartram flew over the dying horse's head and landed in a heap. It was not obvious at first what had happened. To everyone but Isla, that is.

She held the weapon up and waded across the creek, unmindful of its coldness. Her risen temperature and rising blood pressure shut the cold out. She knew the horse was dead because she had shot it with the intention of killing it. What concerned her was the condition of its rider who still had not moved. Jake Meadows and one of the trail riders got to their boss first. Before Jake dismounted, he called to Isla.

"Stop where you are if you want to live another minute."

"Don't be stupid, Jake, I didn't shoot your boss, just his horse. He's probably knocked out and needs some attention, so get out of the way and let a woman look at him. He's not one of your precious steers."

Isla moved quickly to Bartram's side and checked for obvious injuries. No bones were sticking out but a knot was forming on the right side of the rancher's head.

"Some bruises and maybe a fracture, but nothing alarming. However, I don't like that knot rising on his head. He could have a bad concussion there. Be careful when you transport him. I recommend a wagon with some bedding in it. And get rid of the horse.”

The conversation was interrupted by Frank Jamison who was riding hell-bent toward them. He was screaming at the top of his lungs, but with all the cattle rounding-up noise, it was hard to understand what he was yelling. He rode straight to Isla, oblivious to the scene in front of him.

“Isla, come quick. Alex is bad hurt. He was caught up at the edge of the rush of cattle and is cut and bruised something awful. I think he may have broken bones or cracked ribs. He’s bleeding and crying out something awful. Good God, what happened here? Did you kill Bartram?”

“Later, I probably will wish that I had but don’t worry, that troublemaker will be fine. Take me to Alex, or better yet, bring him to my place in the wagon.”

“Yes, I’ll do that. Should have thought of it. I’ll be right back. Oh, are you okay?”

“I guess, considering. If Jake can holster his gun and take care of his boss instead of threatening to kill me.”

Jake muttered something under his breath, but put his revolver away and called for two of the cowhands to come help him.

Frank turned his horse and retreated at the same pace he had arrived at.

Isla spoke to the foreman again, "Take Bartram home and let his daughter look after him and take those dad-blamed cattle with you. Get some ropes and pull these dead cows out of the creek, and be thankful that God stayed my hand or more than cattle and horses would be on the ground. And, Jake, one more thing. Don't come back!"

Isla turned around and waded across the creek. She quickly stripped her bed and threw an old cover over the mattress. She stoked the smoldering fire from the morning and added a couple of sticks of wood. She took the kettle, which was already full of water for lunch coffee and set it on the range top. There were precious few cloths but she gathered what she had together. She made a side glance at the cobwebs and proceeded to retrieve them and put them in a spread-out wad on the table. She had been right about those.

She did not take time to look at herself, neither did she think about it. As soon as the water began to heat, she started gathering knives and other instruments, which she put on the table next to the cobwebs. She didn't know what she would need, so she put nearly every tool she owned out. Nothing to do then but wait. She opened the door, unconcerned about the cold air. She wanted to see the wagon coming and she wanted to be there to help Frank bring Alex in.

She remembered to pray. It was easy to pray for Alex but hard to pray for Bartram. Then she thought of what she had done. *Certainly not the peacemaker, are you Isla? Lost your temper and your good sense and to what gain? Cain was wrong and so were you. Pain, broken relationships and guilt overflowing water which is provided freely to all by the God of heaven. Everyone proved their point and two people are injured and peace is lost and you are back to the beginning place.*

The self-criticism continued and with it came tears of fear for Alex and remorse for her part in whatever had happened to him. She was tapping her left foot and gripping her hands together as she strained to see the trace. She stood up and went to the door. The men and livestock were gone. Several dead steers and one horse lay up on the northern bank. She could not see Roy and her cows but she had little interest in them at the moment.

"Dear God, hurry them up, please. Give me wisdom and knowledge, God. Forgive me for I have truly sinned. Like David, give me a clean heart. Guide my hands with the healing of Jesus. Hurry them up, Lord. Ease Alex's pain. Don't let him hate me, Lord, not dearest Frank either," was spoken out loud, soft and earnest and from a broken heart.

Then, it was there. The wagon came to the bottom of the lane, moving very slowly. At first, she was surprised based on the way Frank had been flying about. Then she realized that Alex must be in such pain that he could not tolerate moving faster than a slow walk. She moved out the door. Her right hand wiped her eyes. She was not a crier but she had cried, mostly at the senselessness of the week's events that culminated in the morning's disaster. It had been, after all, a tragedy in the making.

The buckboard stopped as close to the door as possible. Two people were on the single seat behind the board. Isla was shocked to see Deloris rising from off the wagon's bench and preparing to climb down. *Does she know about her father*? I'll *ask later.*

Frank jumped down on the other side and motioned for Isla to help him move Alex. He had placed his brother in the wagon bed on a large blanket. He motioned for Isla to grab one side of the blanket so they could slide Alex out and carry him inside. Isla could not move; she just stared, temporarily paralyzed in shock.

Alex's clothes were nothing but tatters, blood seemed mixed throughout the tatters and on his skin. His face was pale and sweat ran the length of his face from top to bottom. The sounds coming from his lips were horrible moans of pain and his face twitched and his mouth opened and closed. She spoke to him and his eyes fluttered. He moved his lips but nothing understandable emerged.

Deloris also joined Isla and Frank in lifting and sliding the blanket and Alex out of the buckboard. She had not bothered to wipe her tears which was just as well as they continued to seep down her cheeks. She had seen wounded cowhands before but this was different. It was Alex that was hurt, and it was her father who had caused it and she couldn't reconcile the truth of the action and reaction. She could only think of how different the young, wounded Alex was from the man her father had become. The tears flowed harder and she unsuccessfully smothered a moan of her own.

Slowly the trio eased Alex and the blanket through the doorway and into the small bedroom. Frank began to cut Alex's tattered pieces of cloth free with his pocket knife. Alex yelled as the cloth pulled away from the drying sticky blood. Isla went to the living area for cloths and hot water. She was followed like a shadow by Deloris.

"How can I help you, Isla?"

"You take the wagon to the Jamisons' place and ride your horse home and see about your father, Deloris. He needs you. He may need you a lot."

"What happened?" The tears stopped and her expression changed from worried to alarm.

"I shot your father's horse and when it stumbled, your father flew off head first and hit the ground. He's alive but left here unconscious. Your cowhands took him somehow. I'm sorry. I'm so very, very sorry. This never should have happened and wouldn't have happened if I hadn't been determined to stand up for my rights as a woman by acting like a man."

Deloris looked towards the bedroom and back at Isla. "I think I love Alex; what should I do?"

"Frank and I will take care of Alex. Your father needs you. You need him. Go, child. Send us word when you know something."

Deloris looked in at Alex, choked up and then ran out the door to the buckboard. In the background, Isla heard it leave, gaining speed with every stride of the elderly Morgan.

She and Frank washed Alex as clean as possible and Isla began her inspection of the damages. There were various lacerations and multiple bruises. She gently touched Alex's left side and he screamed out. She had to feel for internal injuries in spite of the protests. The ribs were definitely injured. Maybe one or two broken and the others badly bruised, maybe even minute cracks.

Isla took an older sheet and ripped it into wide strips. With Frank's help the two of them wrapped the chest area as tightly as they could. Alex passed out, but Isla thought that was a good thing because she was about to clean out two deep lacerations made by horns or hooves. Either way, there was the danger of infection and there was not much available to stop infections twenty-five miles from civilization.

She took her strong, homemade soap and reheated the water. Slowly, carefully, she put the water and soap in the wounds and then wiped them out. When she was satisfied, she dried them off with a softer cloth. She left the room and returned with the cobwebs in her hand. Using a wooden spoon, she spread the cobwebs into the openings, packing as much in as she had available.

"We'll take turns watching Alex and doing the chores, okay?" she asked.

"Thank you, Isla. I could never have done that. The war was one thing, but Alex is my flesh and blood. Do you think he will be okay?"

"I think so, but it won't be overnight. It won't be a few days, either. Hopefully, just weeks. We need some help. When I know he's stable, I'll go to Cheyenne and find Second John. I won't take no for an answer."

Frank nodded and then the gates burst. The tears and anger he had been holding back came free at last. He lowered his head as his back shook uncontrollably.

"I may shoot that man if he lives."

"No, Frank. You will forgive him and me. I'm to blame as well. I forgot the importance of being a peacemaker and instead, I have brought pain. We will try to do no more harm but we will do good."

She put her arm around his shoulder and pulled his head close against her. The tears continued to flow. Frank shook his head. Another Isla of the several he had already met. He would think about it. He didn't blame her, couldn't blame her, but he could blame August Bartram and that was what he was doing, for the moment at least.

Frank pulled the small bedside chair up next to Alex and placed his hand on an un-bruised spot of his brother's arm. He bowed his head and alternated crying and cursing. But the cursing was under his breath. He would not let Isla hear the words after what she had just said.

Isla went into the living area and began the cleanup. There was a lot to throw away, for she felt no desire to restore such bloodied cloths. In a few minutes, she had things put away and cleaned to her satisfaction. She began looking at the new supplies to determine what she might fix for a simple lunch if they grew hungry, that is. Life had to go on. Good or bad, it must go on. *I can decide which*, she reasoned.

She checked on the livestock and Roy. She found
Balloch and brought him to the back by the chicken
coop and brushed him down. She re-fed the chickens
and looked at the baby chicks. She examined her
cellar work and reaffirmed her need for a cow shed.
She looked at the dead flowers and dying shrubs and
turned away. Enough of that.

She walked down to the creek's edge and looked at her
reflection. It startled her. She looked older and sadder
and how she felt, depressed. It was not Isla. Not Isla at
all. She straightened up and squared her shoulders.
She thought of her hard-working mother and the
perseverance of her family. *What would they think of
her if they saw her today?* She quick-stepped to the
house and put a meal together. Not a snack nor a feast
but a meal. The march of the sun had fooled her as
she had no concept that the day had progressed so
rapidly.

NINE

Half a day's journey towards Ft. Laramie, a small struggling band of Arapahos made their way south, occasionally using the stagecoach road to ease their journey. There were three young braves, five young squaws and various children and elderly in the party. Their group had been decimated by a strange disease they may have contracted from white men near the fort. Because of the extended delay the disease had caused, they missed the major buffalo migration south.

They were trying to catch up but due to their physical condition, they were actually falling farther behind. Without divine interference or a stroke of extraordinary good fortune their prospects of surviving the coming winter were indeed dim. The oldest of the young men wanted to go scout ahead but he was overruled. The entire band felt a need to stay together and lean on the Great Spirit and their own uncanny ability as a people to survive in the most primitive conditions. They were a proud people but they were also hungry and there were children and the old ones.

They would reach Buffalo Creek an hour before dark.

Frank was amazed at the lunch, but due to the stress of the morning's events he really couldn't concentrate on it.

"Thank you, Isla, I know this took time and we sure needed it. But I have to confess that I'm having trouble thinking of anything but Alex and my feelings for Bartram. I'm so behind on the store I'm afraid I won't be ready for the colder days coming. You can't keep Alex in your bed and sleep on the floor and you have work to do of your own. It's overwhelming. I don't know how you are coping with it all."

"I wasn't, Frank. I was too busy to cope. I saw myself in the creek, that's all. It wasn't Isla McNeese at all and neither is the man sitting across this delicious meal Frank Jamison. It's bad but not the end of the world and we have help unseen. You will make it and so will Alex and I'm definitely a survivor. Tomorrow will be better or if not, the next day will. I have your back just like you had mine. Go do what you can and as much as you can. Alex and I will be fine, I promise."

Frank looked at the lady in front of him. He hadn't really noticed the toll the morning had taken on her. He had been thinking of Alex and had not really thought about what Isla had done to Bartram and his cattle and how it might be affecting her. He stood up and walked to her chair.

"I'm sorry, Isla. I was thinking about me and not you. Please forgive me. I really appreciate all you do. You are a special person whom God has put in my life for some reason even if I'm too busy to notice it. I'm going to work hard and trust you and God."

Isla reached up and touched his hand. It was one of the few times she or he had shown much physical attachment. It was like a shock and she quickly withdrew it. This was not the time she reasoned. Frank, similarly affected, moved in long strides to the door. He grabbed his hat and left before he said or did something that would be foolish.

Once the kitchen chores were finished, Isla checked on Alex again. She changed one bandage and felt his head. It was hot but not as hot as it was earlier. He needed more help than she could give him, but what was there to do? *It's in your hands, God, I've got work to do.*

Isla closed the cabin door and grasped the large pan in her left hand using her hip as an aide. In the pan were her best knives. She would skin the best-looking steer and try to salvage as much beef as she could, especially the liver. What to do with the rest? Frank and she would have to use Maude to haul them as far east across the road as possible. The flies would soon cover the carcasses and disease would follow. She was thankful for the cool weather which would slow the decomposition but she found a drop of sweat on her brow just the same.

She wasn't sure exactly how to go about it, but she figured she would build a fire by the steer and rig up a pole and begin smoking the meat as she cut it away. It was the only way she knew to preserve it in the semi-cool air. She had heard stories of how it was done, but it would be a trial-and-error effort driven by necessity. She had eaten beef jerky and knew it was not only good but very sustaining. It would have to do. Maybe if she worked it out fast enough, she could save one other of the smaller steers as well.

The last of the meat was hanging over the smoky fire when she heard the sound of horses and shuffling feet. Joints aching, she turned to the east and the road. She shook her head. Just what she needed. More trouble and she had left her rifle in the house, not wanting to see it again that day.

One of the three riders broke away from the group and slowly, cautiously, approached her holding up an open palm. She wasn't sure if the young brave was afraid of her or afraid of making her afraid. She did not speak but stood straight up with her hand in a similar figure. She was much taller than the brave; that was obvious even with him mounted. He showed his first stolid face break. He was taken by surprise by the tall female figure standing in front of him with a large butcher knife in her right hand.

The Indian pointed to the nearest dead steer. "You trade?"

"No, not trade," she said, moving her hand back and forth and her head shaking side to side slowly.

"My people are hungry. We have old and young. We must eat. I give you good wares."

"No, no trade. Your people may take all of them across the road and down the hill. All of them. I give." She pointed to the steers and put her hand over her heart. Then she motioned with her hand to the other side of the stagecoach road.

The brave fought to keep his dignity, but the relief was on his face just the same. The miracle they had asked the Great Spirit for stood in front of him. He did not trust white people nor did he really want anything to do with them but...this must be done and it was not of his doing.

He nodded. He motioned to the sky and swept his hands across the arc of heaven. He allowed a small smile to slip. Then he wheeled his pony and giving a hoop that shattered the quiet fall of dusk, sped towards his band, waiting hopefully along the water's edge by the ford in the road. In moments the entire group were speeding across the grass, forgetting in the excitement how exhausted and depressed they were. Knives flashed and skin flew. Isla stood fascinated. The skins went on the ground and then carefully cut up portions went on the skins. Little was left on the grass for the circling birds.

The skins were folded and loaded on the horses and the group vanished across the road as silently and quickly as they had arrived.

Isla stood still, not moving during the entire process. Then it dawned on her that her prayer had been answered and maybe someone else's. It also dawned on her that dark was upon her and Maggie needed milking.

She was halfway through getting the milk down when horses came up behind her. It was difficult to see as the moon was still getting into the darkening sky but Carla called out to reassure Isla she was safe.

"Ryan and I are here, Isla. We just heard what happened. We're so sorry. We've come to offer help. How is young Alex? How are you and Frank? What can   we   do?"

Isla slowed the flow of milk, trying to concentrate in the growing darkness. *What was needed most?*

"Give me a minute. Please go into the house and light the candle on the table. I'll be in as soon as I put the milk in the cellar to cool."

The candle cast shadows across the main room. Low groans escaped from the bedroom. Carla was fixing coffee and Ryan stepped across to peer in on Alex. Isla dropped into the empty chair, the whole day suddenly falling in on her. The tears came and then the shakes.

"I'm sorry," she managed to say between sobs. "I've held it back all day."

Carla moved to put her arms around her distraught neighbor.

"It's okay. We are here to help and we will help. In a minute, when you're ready, we'll talk."

Ryan stepped back into the living area. "My goodness, what a mess. How did this happen? What in the world happened here? Do you know anything about A.B.?"

"Sit down, Ryan, and be quiet. Men! In good time all will be known but now we must wait."

Ryan acknowledged his mistake and took the remaining chair. Then he got back up and poured himself a cup of coffee. He looked longingly at the cup wishing he had some brandy to add. *He needed more than coffee, he thought. What had happened to his quiet prairie?*

A brief knock on the door announced Frank's arrival. He had seen the extra horses and was prepared for the scene before him. That is, all but Isla crumpled on the table. He went into Alex's room and got the fourth chair. He was aware that it was a time for silence, so he said nothing, although he was full of questions.

Isla looked at Ryan and then at Frank. "I know you don't want to just sit here, so why don't you two men go across the creek and take care of the beef jerky I'm smoking before it gets too dark or the coyotes get it. When you come back, we'll figure out what we should do between the four of us. I don't think Deloris will be much help at this point."

"Carla, there are lots of leftovers from a fabulous lunch that went uneaten," Frank offered, "perhaps you would be so kind as to fix us all a plate. We'll think better on fuller stomachs and thank you for the coffee. I needed it. I'm very needy, I think, at the moment."

Frank and Ryan rode across the creek and retrieved the beef jerky. Little was said during the meal, but hundreds of questions and answers were on four lips. Somewhat fuller and calmer, Isla launched into the inevitable discussion.

"I'm going to tell you what happened as far as I know, and then I want to share what I think needs to be done in the now and maybe for the short future."

The rest nodded and slowed their eating to match their curiosity and concern. Every eye was focused on Isla and every eye relayed their strong feelings for such a woman of courage.

Isla ended her account with the interruption of milking. Little was said during her recounting of events but some under-breath sounds were emitted with the telling of the traveling Indian family and the disposal of a serious problem.

"Here is what I propose. First, we need to check on Mr. Bartram and Deloris. We know nothing about the seriousness of his injuries or even if he is alive. Second, Frank has to have some help with his buildings or all will be lost. Third, someone needs to sit with Alex so I can go to Cheyenne and get help. We can't make it without some additional help. I also want to tell the law what happened and have them come out here and see for themselves. I will get some medical supplies and a doctor if I can find one who will come this far. Last, someone needs to talk to the ranch hands and keep them away from my land."

Ryan spoke first as if he had already been deciding things, which no doubt he had. He was a businessman and a successful rancher and he had dealt with emergencies before.

"Carla and I will proceed to the Rocking AB and see what is happening and needs to happen. If needed, Carla can help Deloris. Tomorrow morning, I will send two of my better hands to help Frank catch up. We're not too busy on buildings just yet. Then I will come over here and sit with Alex. I know how to change bandages and feed sick people."

Frank shook his head. It was all unexpected. Moving from despair to hope in a matter of minutes rattled him some.

"If you folks will excuse me, I would like to spend some time with my brother while you plan. I'm overcome with gratitude to you both."

He looked at Isla as if to say, 'You were right,' and took his chair into the bedroom and closed the door. Men don't like to cry in public.

"I'll take care of the food and dishes while you folks go to Deloris. I want to get a really early start in the morning for Cheyenne. It will be a long trip with a wagon. Ryan, could I impose on you to milk Maggie when you come to sit with Alex?" Isla asked.

"Just give me a list when I come in the morning. I'm a good hand with lots of experience with cows, chickens and dogs."

The two Gardeners stood up and this time it was Isla who hugged Carla. She held on for just a minute and then pushed away.

"I'm getting carried away and I don't have time for that. Go on, you two, and be safe in the dark."

TEN

It was still dark the following morning when Isla went outside to saddle Balloch to ride to Frank's. Ryan was waiting outside her house when she exited. She was glad to see him, although she had not expected him so early.

"I thought you might want to hear about the situation at the Rocking AB before you left this morning, so I came early. Just in time, it seems."

"Oh, yes, thank you, Ryan. I am so preoccupied. How is Mr. Bartram?"

"He is alive but in a lot of pain. The tumble from his horse was pretty rough. You must be some shot to hit that horse in motion without hitting A.B. Anyway, he has some broken bones, not sure which or how bad. His jaw is swollen and two teeth are missing. No one knows about internal injuries but he complains of headaches when he wakes up. Jake Meadows left yesterday afternoon for Cheyenne to find a doctor and the sheriff. You can take those off your to-do list."

Isla was in a hurry but the news made her pause. "What about Deloris?"

"Confused. Worried to death about her father and mad as a hornet that he did what he did and concerned about you and Frank and Alex. Torn between her love for her dad and the values she was taught by him and her mother at a younger age. It'll take a while. Carla will help her. She'll be all right and maybe this will bring about a change in A.B. and life can go back to normal on the Buffalo."

"Thank you, Ryan," Isla's voice was barely above a whisper.

Isla saddled Balloch and rode to Frank's. She was surprised to find Maude already harnessed to the buckboard, ready to go. She tied Balloch to the rear of the wagon and climbed on board. She waved to Frank and urged Maude into a quick walk. Cheyenne was too far to trot the entire distance but a nice steady stride would shorten the trip.

Sometime after the sun reached its peak, Isla pulled off the road into a small grove of trees to eat her meal and let Maude take a break. She took a short nap when she finished eating and thus missed the foreman from the Rocking AB as well as the doctor and sheriff from Cheyenne. It was just as well, as that meeting would have slowed her down and she was in no mood to talk to Jake.

It was late afternoon when Isla reached Cheyenne. Isla went straight to the general store where she had first encountered Second John Roberts. He used the store as a makeshift office for people looking for him to do odd jobs. She hoped she would find him and that he would not be so upset at her for not keeping him on before that he wouldn't talk to her.

On the long trip to Cheyenne, she remembered the things Second John had told her about his life on their first trip to Buffalo Creek. Though she discovered later he was not one to volunteer information, he seemed willing that day to answer her questions. The more he told her, the more interested in his life's story she became and so the questions kept coming and Second John kept answering.

Second John had driven the large freight wagon that contained the things for her new house plus a load of lumber. It took several trips to get it all to Buffalo Creek but she only accompanied him on the inaugural one. She kept Balloch close beside the driver's seat so they could talk. Twenty-five miles with a freight wagon was a long trip and she wanted to know something about the man who would be sleeping on the ground under the wagon while he framed the house she would finish.

He answered her personal questions without making excuses or bragging, whichever was called for. She was surprised to find a person of his background so willing to talk about the ups and downs of life. Maybe it was the loneliness and growing old with no one to share his life's story with. He had been so open that she had found herself sharing the hard times of her short marriage and her efforts to make a go in what was to her a foreign land.

Her first question, of course, was where did the name Second John come from and why did he still use it?

"Well, ma'am. My daddy's name was John Hanson Roberts and my mother didn't want to call me Hanson and calling me plain John would have been confusing, so she called me Second John."

"How old were you when you left home, Second John?"

"I'd just turned sixteen. There were five of us kids and we all had to work on the sharecropping farm near Jackson. Sixteen seemed as good a time as any."

"You grew up in Jackson, Mississippi?"

"No, ma'am, Jackson, Tennessee."

"Where did you go and what did you do since all you knew was sharecropping?"

"Well, ma'am, a sharecropper fixes and repairs and makes do. By the time I got to be sixteen, I could do lots of things, like repairing plows and harnesses, shoeing horses, sawing wood and hammering nails."

"So, what did you do?"

"I heard there was a big hotel being built in Memphis so I took my horse and saddle, said goodbye to my folks and headed for Memphis. Never looked back or went back."

"You never saw your family again?"

"No, ma'am. Never did. Thing was, it just didn't seem to work out and the way it all went, I would have been ashamed to go back."

"What do you mean by that?"

"I was too young and all of the men working on that hotel were older than me. They taught me a lot of things I didn't know about carpentry and pipefitting and such, but they taught me a lot of things that wasn't so good."

Isla thought about what Second John had just said. It was wisdom based on experience but she sensed that whatever it was he had somehow overcome it. She wanted to hear the what and how, but it seemed like it was being invasive in someone's private past that might best be forgotten.

"Do you ever talk about it, Second John? Are you embarrassed or ashamed of what those men got you into?"

"Only if someone asks me and someone seldom does. But, no ma'am, I'm not ashamed now, just sorry. Like I said, I was only sixteen and didn't know much about the world but sharecropping. Memphis was a bad town. Not like Jackson."

"So, what kind of things did you get into that caused you trouble? I grew up in the country near a small town in Scotland and very few bad things ever happened."

"I guess it started with the drinking. We worked long hours on the hotel and we'd stop by a saloon on the way to the boarding house. First, it was a beer and then more beers and then whiskey and then there were the girls and I didn't know nothing about those kinds of girls."

"What happened with the girls?"

"I bought them drinks and things and they took me home with 'em. Looking back, it was the ruination of my life. I couldn't keep off the alcohol or the girls and by the time the hotel was finished, I didn't have any more money than when I got to Memphis."

"What did you do next?"

"I was a good worker. That's one thing I can say. That life I was living didn't interfere with my work, so the company that built the hotel kept me on. We went up to St. Louis to build another hotel. I thought I could stay out of the bars and away from those kinds of women, but I couldn't. I kept working on hotels and banks and drinking and whoring till I met Maude. I fell in love with her and we moved in together and she put an end to the ladies' part. I still drank a little, well maybe more than a little and I found another bad habit."

"Did you ever marry Maude?"

"No, ma'am. She never put in to do it and I didn't either. We met when I was forty and stayed together until I joined the Rebel army. I was about fifty when the war started."

"What was the new bad habit you picked up and how did that happen?"

"Gambling. Cost more than the drinking and whoring. Forty years old and nothing to show for it but Maude. If she hadn't worked and took care of her money, we wouldn't have made it."

"What was your war experience like and what happened with you and Maude when the war was over?

"I went back to Memphis and joined up when the war broke out. I served as a private in a Tennessee Volunteer group and we fought in most of the Tennessee battles and Missouri too. It changed me. I lost the taste for drinking, gambling, and women. I saw some horrible things. It was God awful...excuse that. Somehow I survived Shiloh, although I don't rightly know how."

"So, you didn't go back home to Maude? Where did you go, back to building hotels?"

"No, ma'am, I didn't go back. I never heard from her and I guess I fell out of love with her and women in general and booze and all that meaningless stuff. Never had another woman, gambled or drank since the war ended. That war took the life out of me."

"What did you do? I know from what you've said that you could do lots of jobs. Did you find something that you liked?"

"I wouldn't say that exactly. I found something I could do and it got me from Tennessee to Wyoming and I'm happy about that. It was honest work and it paid good and the pace suited me and I met some people who were as unhappy about the war as I was."

"You wound up in Cheyenne. Did your job have something to do with the Transcontinental Railroad?"

"Yes, the Union Pacific was desperate for workers. They hired me to drive their 'fix everything wrong' wagon. I drove that wagon all the way from eastern Nebraska to Cheyenne, following the railroad as they were laying track."

"The UP went on west from Cheyenne, why did you stay?"

"Age catching up on me. I fell off a roof and wasn't able to travel with the crew. Still crippled from that."

"What did you do?"

"I picked up odd jobs as people knew about what I could do. Things like helping you, Miss Isla. It's slowed up now. I make do. Mr. Williams at the general store lets me hang my shingle out there."

"Are any of your family still alive?"

"I don't know. I don't think so, not my parents or sisters. I know one brother was killed in the war t'wards the end. I don't think about it. It's past and you can't live in the past, good or bad. There's just now. Live now, that's what I do."

Isla remembered how hard he worked getting her started and how exact he was in all he did. She found that she could completely trust him to keep his word about everything. It was sad in a way that in his later years, he had no family to pass on his good traits. She was feeling sorry again that her own selfishness had robbed her of his help. She was about to undo the wrong she did to him if he would let her.

ELEVEN

True to form, Second John was sitting in an old rocker just inside the door of the mercantile building. He saw Isla as soon as she opened the door and surprise passed through his eyes. Her appearance in his makeshift office was unexpected and he was not sure welcomed. He liked her. He liked her a lot but he felt betrayed in a way. He had wanted to work for her and have a real friend. Was she here to see him or to buy some merchandise from the store? He did not speak but acknowledged her with his eyes.

Isla paused in front of him. "It's good to see you, Second John. I'll be quick. The past is past and as you once said to me, you can't live in the past or the future, just the now. I'm here for the now. I need you. I want you to come to the homestead and work for me. I can't pay much, but you will eat good and be comfortable and appreciated. Will you do it?

"I have things I have to do. I have a wagon and I need to get some things and I want you to drive it back for me. I will ride ahead into the night. Things are desperate on the creek and I need to be there and I need you there too."

Second John stood up, holding to the rocker's arms for balance. "I don't know if I can be much good for you, Miss Isla, but I thank you for the offer and if you'll have me, I'll come."

He stuck out his hand but Isla ignored it. She reached out and hugged his neck.

"The buckboard is outside and here is a list of things I need. Load them up while I run a few errands. Oh, and please feed the horse and get extra food for her for the trip back."

Just like that the deal was sealed and Isla left the store, shedding relief every step of the way to the bank. It was getting late so she hurried across the street. Hope against hope. She needed a nice banker and she needed him sooner rather than later. As luck would have it, she met him coming out of the bank building as she was about to step in. A few moments of pleading and the kind old gentleman relented and let her inside. *It was a good omen,* she thought.

Her next stop was at a large lumber yard next to a rail spur. The yard seemed low on lumber and she felt a sinking feeling within. Maybe not such a good omen. Back straight, she walked through the door, a letter of credit from H. J. Rogers & Company in her hand. It was not as bad as she had thought.

"No, ma'am, I can't fill this size order today, but we are expecting several flat loads of lumber in the next two days. If you want them hauled out to your homestead, it'll cost extra but with this much lumber, it'll take you several trips in a light farm wagon. We can bring it all on a large freight wagon. Would that work?"

"Yes, sir, it will work. Here is a map to my place. Take what you need from the credit slip and I'll be out of your way with heartfelt thanks. Nice doing business with you."

Isla couldn't believe her luck or was it luck? Anyway, all four items on her hastily drawn-up list were taken care of. She hurried to the general store to help Second John. No need to hurry for the wagon was loaded with lumber and medical supplies. The old handyman was standing next to Maude, his hands stroking her mane and his lips near her ears. She seemed to be enjoying his attention and occasionally reached for his shirt sleeve and nipped at it with her teeth and gums.

Isla stopped short. "You two act like you know each other."

"This is Maude, Miss Isla."

"I know the horse's name, Second John."

"No, Miss Isla, this is my Maude. Named her after that woman I took up with way back. A constant reminder never to do that again. I told this horse she was the only Maude for me. I can't believe you own her."

"I don't, but my neighbors do; we share lots of things, including Maude and the wagon. You think she can handle that load all the way to Buffalo Creek?"

"Maude's a Morgan, Miss Isla. You know what that means?"

"I think I'm about to find out."

"Finest all-around work animal in this country. This lady and I have pulled wagons bigger than this little rig. You ready? I've a hankering to get started on this new adventure and now that I've got Maude for a traveling companion, I'm anxious to get going. I doubled her feed, hope you don't mind. Kept mine the same, but then I'm riding and she's pulling, seems right."

"You're a wise man, Second John. Now, I'll tag along for a few minutes to catch you up on the situation you're getting into. It's bad, but it's going to get better and you are just the man to help me make it better. I'm going to start at the beginning and you can ask questions, although I don't expect you to do more than listen and decide for yourself. Anyway, no secrets, so you feel free to interrupt if you need a clearer picture of what I'm going to tell you. You lead and I'll ride right beside you like on our very first trip to Buffalo Creek."

Isla mounted Balloch just in time to almost get unseated. She barely pulled around the wagon when the sharp whistle of an eastbound train pierced the thin air. Both animals flinched, but neither bolted. It was a familiar sound to Maude and she just snorted to show her disgust at the interruption. She wanted to go home and she wanted to make sure her friend was right behind her.

When Isla was finished with her explanation to Second John, she waited for some comment. It was forthcoming, but not what she expected.

"Good to see you, Miss Isla. I'll hurry. Be careful."

She looked at the old man and grinned. "Same old Second John."

Deloris sat on one side of her father's bed and Carla on the other. The seriously wounded rancher came into consciousness and went out. Mostly he slept but when he woke, he groaned and complained about his head and shoulder. His left arm was tied down so he couldn't move it and it offered less pain. Twice he looked at his daughter and frowned.

"That woman you so admire has nearly killed your daddy. I hope you're satisfied. I'll assure you when I can get out of this bed, I'm getting some satisfaction."

Before either lady could respond, he dropped his head back on the pillow and passed out. The pain his injuries were causing was affecting him, but so was the pain he was feeling inside. *Put to a sick bed by a woman, a foreign woman at that.* It was too much to think about and so he didn't, couldn't. The only recourse from the nearly constant pain was sleep, and so he slept and dreamed and the dreams were as bad as the pain.

Carla looked across the sick bed at Deloris. "I'm sorry, Deloris. Maybe when he feels better, he won't feel so bitter."

"No, Carla, it isn't just today. It's months of missing mother and blaming the wrong person. He's good at that, and until he decides to face the real cause of the pain, he won't change."

"Who does he blame for your mother's death? It was a heart attack. Too much work, not enough help."

"He blames God. Mother was a real believer. No formal church much in this part of the world, but she had her King James Bible and it was thumbed to death. She loved the Lord and taught me to love him as well."

"I thought your dad was a believer."

"He was. Still is, I think, but he denies it. He couldn't take any responsibility for her hard life and frail frame, so he passed it on. He has to say he doesn't believe so he can curse God. He doesn't say that Mother's God is bad, just his."

"You want to take a rest, Deloris? I'll stay here and then we can swap out."

"I guess so, we don't both want to wear out the first day and night."

"Deloris, do you know where Jake is? I called for him earlier to see about your dad's horse and the men said he was gone. He left as soon as he put your father in the bed."

"Jake's assistant, Jamie Lee, told me Jake went for a doctor and the sheriff. Jake's got a fast horse, so maybe the doctor will get here tomorrow morning, if he will come out this far."

"Jake won't give him much choice, I don't think. It would also be good if the sheriff comes and can settle this down before too many stories circulate. I hope he's a peace officer and not a jailer."

Balloch stopped two feet short of the small hitching rail next to the cabin door. His rider was holding his reins in one hand and the saddle horn in the other. She almost lost her grip when he stopped, but managed to hold on long enough to right herself and get a foot out of a stirrup. She slid to the ground and began to remove the saddle. Balloch did not move nor did he want to. Somehow Isla got the saddle off and leaned it against the edge of one of the rail's posts.

Next came the soft wool blanket, now somewhat wet, like the sides of Balloch's flanks and stomach. She rubbed him down, whisking away as much of the lather and wetness as she could. Her back ached as did her arms, but this had to be done. It was growing colder in the early morning hours and she could not let the sweat dry on Balloch's skin and give him a chill. When she finished, she put her arms around his neck and then kissed him on his forehead. He did not move, but she felt he knew. She grabbed his mane and turned him towards the creek.

"Go find your buddy, Roy, and go to sleep. You're my pride and joy, Balloch, and no horse more gallant."

Isla opened the door to the living area and stepped into the dark room. It took a moment to get her bearings in the dark. Snores came from the bedroom and from the pallet on the floor. She had forgotten about Ryan.

Where will I sleep?

She stepped forward and bumped into a table chair. She pulled it out and sat down. It was the only choice. She was too tired to care. She knew, like Second John,

that she couldn't live in the past or the future, there
was just now. She folded her arms across the table
and lay her head down, making a slight adjustment
for comfort and fell into a deep sleep without dreams.

TWELVE

Her first sense of morning came with the smell and sound of boiling coffee. She tried to open her eyes but they were just thin slits. She could see the form of Ryan next to the small wood stove and mixed with the growing smell of coffee was the odor and sound of sizzling salt pork bacon. She glanced to her left, yes, that was a saucer of leftover bread spread smoothly with yellow butter. It looked so good, but she couldn't make her arms move to pick it up.

No words were spoken but a cup of coffee and a small jar of cream appeared directly in front of her. Her eyes opened more. Just enough to see Ryan cracking eggs into a frying pan on the back burn plate. She watched as he broke the yokes and turned them over. The strong scent of bacon grease joined the other vapors rising from the warm stove. *The heat is lovely,* she thought.

She picked up the coffee and moved it to her lips. The rim of the cup was hot and the coffee hotter. Too hot to drink, but maybe in a minute, not too hot to sip. She made the reach for the bread and broke a piece off. Ryan said nothing and neither did she. She was not yet capable of speech. Her mouth was dry and filled with the taste of unwashed beef jerky. *Thank you for the jerky, but I need a drink.*

She tried the coffee. Still too hot, but she took a sip anyway to wet the bread. Ryan moved towards her and a plate of eggs and bacon stopped a few inches away accompanied by a metal fork. She just stared and then she looked up at Ryan's face. *This is a good man,* she thought. She picked up the fork and stabbed a piece of egg. *Goodness, it was so good.*

Ryan sat across from her, a plate and cup of his own. "When you're ready," he said. And so it was quiet except for the chewing and metal ware on the plates. The sun was making more light through the front window and then the sound of the red and yellow rooster put an end to the silence. The day had begun and all the work that came with it and she could not move.

"Thank you, Ryan. This is the best thing anyone has done for me in a long time. Carla is a very lucky lady. How is Alex?"

"The same, I think. Nothing worse. Temperature up and down. Less moaning, which I hope is a good sign. Hopefully, the doctor will tell you more when and if he gets here. If you're able, I would like to hear about the trip. Did you hire Second John and is he on the way?"

"Yes, Second John and his beloved Maude are traveling through the night. I expect him not long after the chores are done. He has a starting load of lumber and some medical things."

"Beloved Maude?"

"Yes, turns out he was the previous owner of Maude. They go back aways evidently."

"That's something. Did you see the banker I recommended?"

"Yes. He was extremely helpful, especially after I mentioned that you personally sent me to him."

"I thought that might work, we do a lot of business with H. J." And the lumber for the rest of the barn?"

"Ordered. They can't keep it in stock. They are expecting a large rail shipment in the next couple of days and they promised to send it up by a freight wagon as soon as it was unloaded and reloaded. They're frustrated because the demand is higher than the supply. There will be an extra delivery charge because of tying up loaders and a wagon team for the long round trip, but there was no choice but to pay it."

"You need to get some rest. Lay down and go to sleep for an hour or so."

"Can't. Got too much to do and there is only one of me, although a rather large one of me."

"I will do all the morning chores. You clean up and rest. There's a pot of water on the left burner in the back. You'll feel better."

"Probably look better, too. I'm covered with road dirt. I have to fix Frank's breakfast."

"Did you fix mine?"

She looked at him and gave the first hint of a smile. "Got me. He's not an invalid, is he? I will take your advice, but I can't rest long. Second John is coming and I have to get him squared away. He'll be exhausted and he may need the pallet for a while. What are you going to do?"

"When I finish here, I will ride over and sit with Carla and Deloris. The sheriff will have been there and maybe the doctor. I can get caught up with the news. You better plan on staying in the house, it's getting colder outside, I can tell, and you're going to have company before lunch. The sheriff and doctor will be here, I'm sure, and they aren't coming to see me. Have you thought about what you will tell the sheriff?"

"Yes, of course. The truth. Could I have another cup of that delicious coffee and maybe some water? I'm dry from mouth to toes."

"Sure. My father used to tell me when I worked too hard, 'Son, if you don't take care of yourself, you will be no help to others when they need you.'"

"You're right. I mean your father was right but, but…"

"You have help, Isla. Let someone else help you so they can have the joy you get when you help them. I'm gone. Lay down. I'll stop and tell Frank to give you some time to rest. I'm sure he has plenty of things to occupy his time before he cooks his own breakfast."

Isla nodded and managed to pull herself up from the table and chair. Ryan took her arm and guided her over to the edge of the pallet. "See you this afternoon and hopefully with some good news for a change."

Thirty minutes later, Frank quietly entered the stove-warmed house and peeked in at his sleeping brother. He looked at the floor and smiled at the dead-to-the-world superwoman. His movements were slow and deliberate to avoid waking either of the two sleepers. He ate his meal thinking of all the events swirling around his life in the middle of a prairie in southeastern Wyoming. One thing he did know, he was in love with the superwoman sleeping on the floor so his injured brother could be in a bed.

Frank left everything where it was. He knew she would move it later and he wanted his departure to be as quiet as his arrival. He looked at Isla once more and felt a strong desire to walk over and bend down and kiss her forehead. He shook his head. Wrong time. She's too tired for an emotional shock and she needs to rest. Later, later, but not too much later.

The two men just missed each other; Frank turned into his place at the same time Second John came in view of the little homestead he had helped start. His eyes took in everything as he and Maude made their way up the very slight incline. He was surprised to be met by a medium size wiry-haired dog barking and circling the wagon. He spoke to the little guard dog, but to no avail. Roy had learned to ignore Frank but here was a stranger, although he did recognize Maude. Roy thought he might just trot along and see what would happen.

Second John drove past the cabin to just beyond the chicken house. He wasn't sure where the barn would be located so he braked the wagon and began the un-harnessing. For lack of better information, he lay the horse collar and reigns across the roof of the chicken coop. When the unhitching was completed, he slapped Maude playfully on her rump and sent her towards the water as he knew she was as thirsty as he was.

When he turned around, he saw a strange man coming from a newly dug root cellar. Roy left watching Second John and ran towards the newcomer. The man leaned down and whispered to the dog who immediately turned and ran towards the creek.

"You must be Second John," the stranger said. "I'm Ryan Gardener, Isla's southside neighbor. Just taking over her work while she went to find you. Want help unloading that lumber?"

"Thank you, sir. Where does it go?"

"I think we'll stack it by the chickens. I know she wants all the buildings in this area, so it'll be close and not in the way."

"That your dog?"

"No, Isla's. Smarter than most humans around this creek."

Ryan asked questions about the trip and the weather and other small talk and Second John gave polite, short-word answers. Ryan soon got the message and the unloading proceeded quietly. When they were done, Ryan walked over to the now famous Second John and extended his hand.

"Welcome to the creek, Second John. I expect Isla will be calling you for breakfast in a few minutes. She is a pretty worn-out lady and I told her to rest, but Roy's greeting to you no doubt woke her up. I'm going up to see my wife at the next ranch. You can expect company soon because both the sheriff and a doctor are headed this way, probably before lunch."

"Yes, sir."

Ryan shook his head and went to find his horse and gear. Second John walked to the creek and knelt down and drank his fill. He wiped his mouth with his denim shirt sleeve and walked back to the now empty buckboard. He pulled his tired body onto the bed and stretched out. He was hungry, but he was more in need of a straight sleep.

Isla found him an hour later sleeping soundly in the cold on the springboards of the wagon. She shook her head. *Why not come in the house, dear friend? We're family now.*

She touched him gently, not wanting to startle him. He moved up on one elbow and smiled. "Morning, Miss Isla. I'm hungry."

"Come inside, I have eggs, bacon and coffee with your name on them."

"Yes, ma'am. I washed in the creek."

THIRTEEN

The sheriff and his deputy had arrived at the Bartram ranch early the previous evening and Jake made a place for them to spend the rest of the night in the bunkhouse.

"I'll come get you gentlemen up after beans. You might want to talk to a few of the hands that were at the creek, so I'll have them hang around after they eat. We got a lot of work to do, but they'll want to help clear this mess up."

"I have a question or two for you, Jake."

"Yes, sheriff."

"Why were you pushing the cattle across the creek? Is that the normal routine for watering the stock?"

"No, sir. We usually just drive them near the water and they wade in and out as they have need."

"So, why the..."

"Mr. Bartram's orders, sheriff. He told us to push them hard, across the creek by the Scottish woman's buildings."

"I see. Hmm..."

"Jake, I suggest that you and your cattle stay as far away from your neighbor as possible today. Either don't water the livestock or move them out of her sight and mine too."

"That's our plan, sheriff. We've had enough for one day. Maybe several."

The law officers waited for an hour after breakfast before approaching the front door of the ranch house. Their questioning of the three riders told them about what they expected, little or nothing, since they had their hands full of thrashing cattle. Would August Bartram be able to shed any light on the incident was the question? He arrived late to the creek, from what Jake told them and was out of the picture before he even reached the herd.

An attractive, petite middle-aged lady answered the door and invited them in. "I'm Carla Gardener, a friend and neighbor. Mr. Bartram and his daughter, Deloris, are in the large bedroom. If you will follow me, I'll take you to them. Mr. Bartram is quite sick and I'm not sure how awake he will be. He's very agitated when he is awake and not too rational. His daughter was here when this started and knows a lot about what happened, but to tell you the truth, I don't think you'll learn much of substance until you talk to Isla McNeese."

Things turned out about the way Carla described them. The four of them talked, the sheriff asking Deloris what she knew. The patient slept, if not fitfully.

"I know your relationship to Mr. Bartram, Miss Deloris, but could you just tell us what you know about yesterday and leave as much thinking out of it as you can. What did you actually hear and see that relates to your father's injury and the death of his horse?"

"I knew daddy and the men planned on taking a large herd of cattle to the creek across from Miss McNeese's buildings and cows. He told me that much. He was very angry with her and wanted to punish her for not giving in to his demands for access to the creek. That's not think, he told me that too. He was very open about it. He hated her for some reason but no one really knows why. He was determined to run her out. My father is a very stubborn man, as I'm sure you already know. He's used to getting his own way and overreacts when he doesn't.

"I heard them shooting their rifles to urge the cattle into a faster pace towards the creek and I jumped on my horse bareback and headed down the road to Isla's. I wanted to get there before my father did. He was in the back somewhere when I ran out. When I rode past the Jamisons' place, I saw Frank Jamison half carrying and half dragging his brother from the land behind their building. The last of our cattle were just passing by a few feet behind them.

"I reined in to see what was wrong. Alex, the younger one, was screaming in pain and his clothes were in tatters. I could see blood, but that was all. I ran in the finished part of their house and found rags and a pot of water. Before I could get out, Frank was gone and Alex was lying on a cot. I looked for Frank but couldn't find him. I figured he went for Miss McNeese. They're good friends. I went back in to see what I could do for Alex, but he was in such pain and covered in blood I was afraid to touch him.

"Frank came back and hitched up the wagon and asked me to help him move Alex onto the wagon bed. I followed them to Isla's house but didn't stay to see what happened because Isla told me to go home and see about my dad, as he was hurt. I asked her what happened and she said, 'I shot his horse out from under him and he had a bad fall.'

"I came home and found daddy lying on the bed. The man who helps cook was pulling dad's clothes off and trying to look at his wounds. I screamed and rushed over to help him. Everything else I know I heard from Jake before he went to get you and he was so angry I'm not sure what he said. I was too worried about daddy and too upset about Alex and I love Miss Isla and I couldn't figure that one out."

August coughed and cried out in pain. His eyes opened and he took in his daughter and the visitors. He spoke to the sheriff: "Arrest that Scottish ... arrest that foreign woman for killing my horse and trying to kill me. If you want to stay sheriff, that is. I..."

He tried to finish but the coughing took hold and Carla pushed him back down on the bed. "Rest, A.B., the sheriff will take care of his business and you can sort it out when you recover. If you don't rest you won't recover very soon if at all. You're a hurt man."

The sheriff and deputy rose and bowed to the ladies. "If you'll excuse us, we'll go pay Miss McNeese a visit now. Don't get up, we know the way out. You'll be hearing from me 'fore long, I 'spect."

Isla and Second John placed string to mark where she wanted to build the new barn and cowshed. "Your room comes first, and then the milking part, and then a stall for Balloch. I think we have enough lumber to start on your half. Which side do you want, quiet side or creek side?"

"Creek."

"Okay, either way, your choice. I measured and consulted Frank and we can build a room about ten feet by twelve. Will that suffice?"

"Yes, ma'am. More'n enough."

"Well, you know what to do. If you need assistance just come get me. Rest when you are tired and I'll call you when Frank comes for lunch."

"Yes, ma'am. I've an eye."

The conversation was interrupted by a streaking, barking Roy on his way to the front of the house. Isla sighed. The sheriff was here and so was the time for truth. She stood straight and tall even though her back still hurt. She put on a brave smile and walked to where the lawmen were dismounting by the hitching rail.

"Good morning, sheriff, I've been expecting you."

"I 'spect you have. You want to talk in the yard or inside."

"Inside, gentlemen. I have fresh coffee and a small sweet cake to share. It's a lot warmer in there and I'm tired and need to sit down if that's okay."

"Sounds good to me," the deputy said and quickly slid to the ground and looped his reins on the rail. The sheriff was right behind him.

This sheriff might be the tallest man I've ever seen. He makes me look like a sprout. Or is it the high-crown Texas hat he's wearing? No, he's tall. He better watch his head on this door frame. I didn't make it for giants. He and that deputy look funny together. He might be the shortest fellow around Cheyenne. Been eating too much and walking too little, I think.

The sheriff wasted no time, which was fine with Isla if not with the short, overweight deputy. The way he lit into the cake was evidence enough.

"Now, Miss McNeese, I need to hear your version of the incident that took place just across the creek that led to a dead horse and a seriously injured man. Could you leave out your thoughts and just tell us what you saw and what you did. Later, if you want to explain something, I'll be willing to entertain that information.

"How did it begin, anyway?"

"For starters, sheriff, it didn't begin yesterday. It began several days ago. I can't tell you the what and why of yesterday without going to the beginning of the disagreement."

"Okay. Let's hear it all, but keep to knowns rather than guesses."

Isla began with her first trip to meet the owner of the Rocking AB. From that, she spoke of the Jamison men and then her visit to the Gardeners. Next came the first incursion of the cattle and her firing shots in the air to make her displeasure known. She told as much of her conversation with rancher Bartram as she could relate, word for word and then mentioned that Frank and Deloris were witnesses to the entire exchange.

"I left embarrassed and angry, but not afraid. I told him what would happen if he trespassed without permission again but he just threatened me more. There was nothing else I could say or do, so I left and came back here. The next morning, I was up early with my rifle waiting because I knew they would come. I didn't expect them to be running the cattle, though, and that frightened me. Several of the steers crossed the river where my dog was trying to keep them back. When they got to the bank, I started shooting. I killed five or six before they turned back.

"The entire herd was milling and thrashing all around the ranch hands who were still firing their rifles into the air. That's when I saw Mr. Bartram racing up the creek bank, waving a rifle in his hand and screaming at his men to drive the cattle into the water. I remembered his personal threat to me. I warned him not to come. He was on my land waving a rifle around and urging his men to drive the cattle on into the water. I was afraid he might shoot me. So, I shot his horse and killed it. I thought the horse rather than the man, although the horse was more noble, I believe.

"At about the same time, my neighbor Frank came riding all out to where I was, yelling that Alex, his younger brother, had been trampled by the cattle and was seriously hurt. I told him to bring Alex to my cabin.

"In minutes, Frank and Deloris Bartram drove into the yard with Alex in the back of the buckboard. He was bad hurt and bleeding. We put him in the bed and I treated him the best I could. He was injured in body and probably in spirit. This was all so unnecessary.

"You can say I was wrong to kill the horse, but you also will have to say that trespassing is against the law and can't be tolerated in a civilized society. Those steers could have done serious damage to my property if not stopped. We do mean to be a civilized society, don't we, sheriff?"

"How did you know you would hit the horse and not the rider, Miss McNeese?"

"You ever shoot at a running deer, sheriff?"

"Shot at them many times."

"How did you know you'd miss them?"

"What? Now see here, my shooting is pretty good."

"But you knew you might miss them. I knew I would hit the horse because I always hit what I aim at. If I had wanted to hurt Mr. Bartram, he would not be in bed at this moment but being prepared for burial. Do you understand what I'm saying?"

"That's a lot of bragging, miss."

"Not bragging, sheriff. Truth. Pure fact and easily demonstrated anytime you need proof. Much like your running deer stories."

The deputy gagged on his second piece of cake and the sheriff's face turned red. He had heard enough in more ways than one.

"I'm going back to Cheyenne and talk to the Territorial Judge. I'll be back in a week or so. I'm going to ask you not to leave the area before I return. I will present the evidence as I've heard it and the judge will decide if we're to have a trial. If a trial, then it will have to wait until Mr. Bartram can testify under oath. So don't leave the homestead and I won't have to arrest you. Is that suitable?"

"Very suitable. I look forward to hearing or meeting his honor. Perhaps he can help me acquire my U.S. citizenship. The time is almost up and I'm ready."

"I'll inquire, Miss McNeese. Thank you for your kind hospitality and cooperation. Come on, cake man."

Isla did not rise. She was too tired and too upset and these were grown men, and not necessarily her friends. When she heard the last of their horses' hooves leave the trace for the hard road she went in and sat down by Alex. He was asleep but it didn't matter. She needed a quiet place to weep the hurt away. In a while, when she was composed, she would go help Second John carry lumber. The sounds of a hammer were already ringing outside the rear of the house.

Past, future, now. I'm doing the now, were her last thoughts before sleep overcame her.

FOURTEEN

Roy barked and the door rattled. Isla wiped her face with a damp cloth, paying close attention to her eyes and cheekbones. She didn't need the mirror. She had cried before. Not for stupidity but for hurt. This was some of both. She practiced her best smile and headed for the door. She swung it open and was greeted by a slight built older man with spectacles and a beard. The beard was about the sum of his hair, but his face looked gentle because of the wrinkles. She knew it was the doctor without asking.

"Come inside out of the wind, doctor, and welcome at last."

"I'm here as soon as Sally would bring me, my dear. Where is the patient? It's been a long trip and we two old-timers would like to be on our way back home. With luck and (cough) Sally's well-known speed, we might make it before too late."

"This way. My name is Isla McNeese, and Alex Jamison, the patient, is a neighbor. I'm sure you've heard the complete sordid details by now. He's in the bed, a slight fever I believe and needs new dressings. I usually do that after lunch. I just made the same trip you did and I, too, am worn out."

Isla opened the bedroom door and allowed the doctor to pass. The elderly physician sat his small carrying bag next to the bed and pulled the thin blanket covering Alex down. Slowly and carefully, he pulled the various strip cloth bandages away from the young man's skin. Alex groaned and then woke up.

"Who are you?" he asked rather brusquely.

"Doctor Otis, Alex. Hopefully a friend in need and in time. How are the ribs?"

"The ribs?"

Doctor Otis gently touched the wrapped bandages.

"Ow! Why did you do that?"

"I needed an answer to my question. Now I have it. You are going to have to bite down on something because I am going to unwrap this cage of yours and see how bad the damage is. Miss, can you get me something for him to grip with his teeth? I'm afraid this pain is unavoidable."

Isla handed him a thick piece of leather, but hovered nearby.

"If you have some outside chores to do, this would be a good time to do them. Alex and I can handle this alone and while he isn't used to it, I am. Say, are there any trout in that creek running by your place? I sure would like some to take home with me."

Isla grinned. "He's tougher than he looks, doctor, and so am I. But if it's fish you want, it's fish you'll get. I've got an empty feed bag I can wet down good and send with you. No warmer than it is they'll keep well. How many?"

"What can you spare, you reckon?"

"Enough for you to finish in here, I think."

"Now there's a bright Scottish lassie if ever I met one."

In minutes, Isla was standing by the bank, wet bag on the bank and fishing line in the water. The sounds of Second John's hammer and saw were occasionally interrupted by yells and groans from the back room. She tried to concentrate on the fishing and block out the noise. The hammering was steady, but the groans were painful to hear.

The fish were in no hurry, which is what she figured the doctor surmised. Slowly, the bag filled with nice-sized fish, the blues on their sides glinting and shining in the near noon sun. They were beautiful fish, these brook trout, but their beauty would not save them in the end. *True for all of us,* she reminded herself, and took one more discouraging look in the water at her face and hair.

The door to the house sprung open and the gentle doctor came across to the creek bank. He held a small piece of paper in his hand and waved it gently in front of Isla.

"I've written a few simple instructions. You'll find the small vial of salve on the kitchen table. I've rewrapped the wounds and the ribs. Two of them are in bad shape. Bed rest for at least one more week and easy does it after that. You probably won't have to remind him but once. By the way, good you had the cobwebs; probably held the infection at bay.

"My, my, you know your fish, don't you, lassie? I'll give you the note in exchange for the bag and wish you a good day."

"Doctor Otis, I have some fresh oats. Please take a cup for your Sally. I'm sure she's more than earned them."

Nothing could have pleased the doctor more. Not even the fresh brook trout.

"I'll bring them out while you load up. Just a minute."

The doctor pulled down the trace with a turn-away wave, Sally already moving into her legendary ground-eating trot. Isla watched for a minute, thankful for such selfless people and went to offer Second John her help.

"That Doctor Otis?" Second John asked.

"The same. Nice man, it seems. I liked him."

"He took care of me."

"That was nice."

"In his house when the hotel ran out."

"That was nicer."

"Yes. I help others to pay him."

"No, Second John, I don't think so. You help others because you're Second John and that's who you'll always be, but at the same time you pay others' debts. You're a good man, Second John, and I'm glad you are joining my family. This is your permanent home now for as long as you want."

Second John donned his usual silence when he was without words which of course was often.

"Can I help you a little before lunchtime?"

"Isn't it?" he answered.

Isla looked at the sky. The sun was way south but not high enough to make noon. Hammering and sawing was hungry work even for a spare man like Second John. The work went fast with two to haul and hold and in no time at all the sun had moved to its noon mark. Isla told Second John to wash up and take a break. She headed for the creek herself and then to the house.

She was starting to feel happy and that was a good sign for the coming lunch crowd. By the time she reached the stove, she was humming Frank's favorite tune. She forgot to be quiet for Alex, but evidently, the exercise with the doctor had worn him out.

Frank opened the door for Second John, who entered and removed his battered old plainsman hat. It had been with him since birth, he had told Isla once. It looked it too. She offered to buy him a new one but he was totally aghast. "Why?" had been his one and only comment and it was enough for her to hear, "No, ma'am." He placed the hat on the top spire of the chair and stood by it, waiting for Isla to sit down.

Isla placed the plates down at their respective seats and poured each of them a cup of coffee. She added a glass of water for herself as she was still feeling dried out from her long trip.

"Your first meal with us, Second John. Would say grace please?" She didn't look at him but bowed her head to avoid an objection.

"Thank you, Jesus," came the prayer.

"Looks wonderful," Frank said. "The doctor saw Alex? What did he say?"

"Changed the bandages, rewrapped the ribs and left some medicine for the cuts. One more week in bed and then light duty for a while. Full recovery expected."

"That's good news. Those two ranch hands of Ryan's are a sight. We are really moving along. It may not be too late to beat the bad weather. By the way, I didn't get to tell you but a northbound stage stopped to speak yesterday. They heard about what we are doing. Wyoming Stage and Transport is currently running two round trips to Laramie and beyond each week. Both towns are really growing, from what the driver told me. They'll shut down the stages mostly in the winter, but come spring, he hears they might well add another coach. If they do, they might use us as a horse changing station for the southbound leg. Build a corral and give Alex a full-time job. How about that?"

"That's real good news for the future. Six stages a week will keep us all busy I'd think with all the other things to do. Good thing you're here, Second John. We'll have to promote you to foreman to manage all the cattle, fish, and chickens we'll need."

The soft-spoken railroader paused and looked up at Isla. "Thank you." Then he turned to Frank whom he very seldom spoke to. "Thank you."

"By the way, Frank, Second John was also at Shiloh during the battle."

Second John looked at Isla and then Frank and shook his head. Frank acknowledged his own desire to bury the past.

Frank went back to work at his place and Second John returned to the barn building. Isla straightened up, checked Alex and lay down on the pallet. A moment of peace swept down the Buffalo and each enjoyed it in their own way.

FIFTEEN

Ryan, Carla and Deloris sat around the large dining table in the big house. There were steaks, potatoes, dried beans and a corn mush dish. They were mostly toying with their meals as each was deep in thought about what their next move would be.

"Things are under control at the Jamisons' and Isla's. They are back on schedule and with luck and a late winter, all will be ready. I need to get the Bar G prepared as well and I've done all I can do here. We're in limbo until we hear from the judge and I don't think that'll happen anytime soon. He will probably wait to hear from A.B., and Isla's a no-run risk. What are your plans, Carla? Coming home with me?"

Carla looked at Deloris. The girl had been subdued since her conversation with the sheriff and the doctor. Doctor Otis had been optimistic as to healing, if not to time.

Carla spoke in a calming voice to Deloris, "This much trauma will take a while and I don't like the head injury or its symptoms. Lots of rest needed there. Lots of it and your dad is not much of one to rest. You'll have to tie him down, Deloris. A brain concussion can be a dangerous thing and your dad is not a spring chicken. Keep him as calm as possible. If he broaches the situation, do all you can to change the subject. Talk about the ranch, the weather and your plans. I assume you have some."

Deloris didn't respond. *Plans, what plans? Stuck miles in the prairie with a very ill father and separated from new friends she wanted to be with.*

She was glad her dad was okay for now, but what about Alex? Ryan had given an update but it wasn't the same. No matter how she thought of it, Alex's injuries and possible future had been the result of her family.

"Not now, Carla, when this is over, maybe. The ranch is the only home I remember much. I guess it is my future."

The sheriff's exchange with her had left her somewhat puzzled. It didn't seem like the sheriff wanted to blame anyone and she was wanting to blame everyone. They all should have backed down and talked. *Grown-ups not as smart as they think sometimes,* she thought. *Maybe the best thing for everyone was to end it now. Bury the hatchet, they say. Let bygones be bygones. They could all be happy. Why couldn't they? Her father, that's why. What could she do to change that?*

Carla knew what was going on in the young head across from her. She had tried to bring some clarity to it all, but Deloris wasn't quite ready for standing up to her dad or herself.

"I'll stay a couple more days and then come home. Deloris is an excellent nurse and will do fine and she has lots of help here. I'll come back every few days and relieve her. I think she wants to make a visit or two anyway. Am I right, Deloris?"

Deloris nodded her head. "I would like to talk to Isla privately. I want her advice on something."

"And that's all?"

"Well, of course, I want to apologize to Frank for my dad's actions and see how Alex is doing."

"Of course. Okay, it's settled. I'll be home in two days and we'll get to work on the coming freeze season."

She followed Ryan to the door and they shared a warm embrace for the first time in a while. The events on the creek had brought them a new insight into their own relationship.

The days turned into weeks and the days grew that much shorter and the sun's warmth that much cooler but the work at the two homesteads moved forward with a sense of urgency, it had to. Second John asked Isla to join him at the first completed section of the barn. The milking part was nearly finished and they were waiting for a last load of lumber for the small horse stall on the south side.

Second John pointed to the base of Isla's house. "The wind's going to come mostly from the southwest and blow on that wall right there. It'll be cold. Not like what you are used to. I want to cut sod and pile it waist-high along the wall. It will stop the wind and keep your bedroom warmer."

"Second John, that is the longest speech I've ever heard you attempt. Are you joining us at the table sessions?"

"No, ma'am. Do it?"

"Do it. Can I help?"

"No, ma'am. Hard work."

"I can do hard work, friend."

"You have Second John for hard work."

Second John cut and stacked sod along the wall. It was almost two feet wide and three feet high. Isla had never seen sod used that way but she trusted Second John and waited till it was finished to comment. She knew he was right because the wall of her bedroom warmed up in the late western sun.

Outside, the chicks were fluffed out and putting on weight. Late arriving hoppers on the creek bank had fattened them all up. Isla doubted there would be another hatch of biddies considering how cold it was. These were doing well and, in the spring, would move to Frank and Alex's house. The cows seemed contented, though starting to spread out farther from the buildings. Roy stayed busy rounding them up. His work with Maggie had ended as Maggie loved the grain at milk time and came on her own. Soon she would spend the night in the barn.

Isla wondered if Roy needed a shelter. Would he leave the cows long enough to get in one? Maybe not now but when the winter weather Second John had been describing to her arrived the dog might have a change of heart. Maybe Roy would move in with Second John.

By her reckoning, Saturday arrived slightly warmer. A nice day for trout to be sure. Isla settled down by the bank and baited her hook. A loud 'hello' broke the tranquil scene. The fisherman looked up and there was Deloris riding at a jog towards her. Isla made no move to get up as she was not sure what territory the visit was in. That quickly changed.

Deloris slid off and dropped the reins. "Hello, Isla, can I visit with you? I've missed you so much. Carla is with daddy and gave me time off. Do you have some time to talk to me?"

"Sure, let me put this stuff away."

"No, I don't want to go inside. I don't want Alex to hear me talking to you. I'm fine, you fish and I'll stand next to you and we can share information."

"Okay. Something is on your mind, tell me."

"Several things are actually, but two really important ones."

"Let's start with the most important one."

"I'm not sure which is at the moment. That's why I want to talk to you."

"Well then, young lady, you pick because I'm in the dark."

"I never got to ask you what happened when you shot my father's horse. You sent me home, remember? It was the right thing to do, I'm sure, but it left me wondering why you didn't offer some explanation of what was going on. What was going on with you? I know about my father. But I don't know about you. Why you did what you did and how did you feel about it?"

"I've thought about it a lot, Deloris. Some of it was stubborn Scottish pride. Some of it was self-determination to be my own person and not be ruled

157

by others, like your father. I did not want to harm anyone, not even a fine horse like your father's. It seemed the only choice I had right then, or be put down by him for the long run. I couldn't make myself give in, but perhaps I should have. Perhaps I should have let him win and lived with the consequences of being under his thumb for the rest of my life here.

"I was angry at your dad. I let his unkind words influence my thinking. I was so angry but I never thought about hurting him or getting even in some way. I just wanted my place and my peace, and he wouldn't let me have it, so I acted in the moment."

"Would you do it again, I mean the same way?"

"Same circumstances, yes, the same way. I wish the circumstances had been different but they were what they were. I acted in the moment. I took no thought of the past or future, I just met the moment. He threatened me and I reacted to that. I'm terribly sorry your dad is bad hurt just like I am that Alex is bad hurt. Can't take it back. We have to leave it to history and move on. That's my plan, is it yours?"

"I'm trying. It's hard. I find no sense or peace in any of it. Things were fine and I met Alex and real joy entered my life. I miss my mother so much and daddy is a busy man. I was very lonely and I was attracted to your handsome neighbor as soon as I saw him. But, now."

"What about now?" Isla asked.

"You know. He disliked my father before this happened and I bet he hates him even more now. He won't want to speak to me. Not in a nice way, anyhow. I don't know if I love him, because I've never been in love, but I do feel something, you know a strong attraction and the injuries have made it worse. I feel like I should be helping him, but I'm afraid he will reject me entirely and if he does, what will I do then? I have no one.

"Before I go any further, I want you to know that I hold no grudge against you. As far as I can tell from what I personally heard and what you and Carla told me, my daddy left you with little choice but to fight or run. He would not have run, I know that. Can we be friends?"

Isla pushed herself up from the cold grass and placed her line-free arm around Deloris' shoulder and pulled her close. "Of course, we will be friends. I would want it no other way. We will be like sisters and love each other in spite of the stupid actions of the other sex. Now, what about Alex?"

"What do I do? Do I go to him and tell him how I feel? Do I wait and see if he comes to me? Dear God, what if he doesn't? I'm lost as to how to go here. Please help me. You know Alex so well. Maybe he's already said how he feels about me. I need to know. I need help Isla, please."

"To be honest, Deloris, I don't think Alex has had the presence of mind nor the energy to think about anything but getting well and enduring the pain of his injuries. Perhaps he's thought of you in some way, but he hasn't mentioned you or much of anything else. He's not a big talker unless he has something to say, and now what he has to say is mostly groans and calls for help.

"But since you asked for my advice, I will give it the best I can. In a few days, pay Alex a social call. Inquire as to his pain. Say you're sorry for what happened. Ask him if you can help in any way. Perhaps you could come read to him a few minutes each day. I'm sure it's quite lonely in that room and the rest of us are mostly working non-stop. See how that goes and then we can reevaluate. You're a lovely girl and he's a lonely boy but don't push. Hear me? Don't rush this, let it occur naturally or not at all.

"He's healed a lot but he is still nursing the hurt. He should be outside by now. Most of the pain is gone. Encourage him to get out of bed and join the rest of us."

SIXTEEN

The intense conversation was suddenly interrupted by the arrival of men on horseback led by the sheriff from Cheyenne. Isla pulled in her fishing line and lay it down on the bank next to the sack containing her morning's catch. She did not move, but it was not necessary since the entire group of men rode right up within a few feet.

"Good morning, sheriff. I've wondered where you've been. Did you bring the entire town with you to capture this desperado?"

The sheriff did not laugh at her little joke nor did he acknowledge Deloris' presence. He was on a mission and wanted it over with.

"I brought the Territorial Judge with me, Miss McNeese. The others came on their own when they heard the reason for our trip."

"And just what is the reason for your trip?"

"I think the judge had better answer that question."

The sheriff made a quick motion to the man just behind him. The judge was older than the rest of the group, but not by a lot. He was dressed in a black suit and white shirt. There was a small black string of some kind hanging around his neck. He was neither tall nor short, thick or thin. Newly gray hair stuck out from under his black fedora. The most outstanding thing about him, Isla thought, were his eyes. They weren't blue or green, but rather seemed to be changing with the light. Most importantly, they seemed to be filled with wisdom. *Good,* Isla thought.

"Good day to you, Miss McNeese. Ordinarily, I would have required your presence in my courtroom but seeing the nature of our inquiry, it seemed more appropriate for us to join you here. At the scene of the, uh, incident, so to speak."

"I see. Well, thank you, your Honor, for sparing me the inconvenience of traveling for two days as we are extremely busy getting ready for the coming winter, and as you can see, we are still in the building and fixing stage of things. Would you care to explain what the nature of the inquiry is?"

"Gladly. It's why the sheriff and I are here, as well as this gang of onlookers who obviously should be employed elsewhere. Maybe they can pitch in and help you since they are already here. Now, Miss McNeese, a great deal of this inquiry happens to focus on your ability to shoot a running horse without injuring the rider or anyone else. That ability has been duly doubted and since you offered to prove it, we are here for the proof. Not to put undue pressure on you, but I must caution you that the validity of your claim of innocence of wrongdoing is based on that proof. Do I make myself clear?"

Isla released her first sigh of relief and a slow smile spread from the corner of her lips.

"Would you get the rifle you used on that unhappy day, please, ma'am?"

Isla nodded and made long deliberate strides toward the house. Deloris ran to keep pace with her.

"Are you scared, Isla? What if you miss?"

"You haven't been listening, Deloris, I don't miss. I know I don't miss. I'm not worried about missing because I am an accurate shot with that rifle. Any other rifle for that matter."

Deloris was not so confident and fearful lines crossed her face. She stopped at the door and waited while Isla went in. *She wanted to say something else but she knew it would be wrong. There was nothing to do but worry. She believed Isla, but anyone could miss once in a while, couldn't they?*

Isla walked back down to the bank and stood in her exact same spot. Slowly she slipped shells into the receiver and levered the first one in. She looked at the judge and nodded.

"I'm ready."

The group of men dismounted and spread along the creek bank for a better view. They didn't know how the test would be conducted but they had come a long way for the show and wanted an unobstructed view.

The sheriff reached into his saddle bag and removed a nearly square foot, flat board. He moved his horse down to the water's edge and prepared to fling the board across to the other bank.

"Sheriff, I don't want to be rude, but I could hit that target with a hand-thrown rock."

"Just hit the target, Miss McNeese. We'll decide about what's needed here," the judge said.

"Your call, throw it."

The block went sailing up and then down but never landed in the water, Isla's bullet cut it in half as it descended. A chorus of exclamations rose from the bank. The judge waved his hand to quieten the onlookers.

"This is a court of inquiry, not a carnival, gentlemen. Hold your noise or I'll have the sheriff remove you from the property. Okay, sheriff, continue as planned, please."

A smaller piece of wood was brought forth and immediately sailed upstream. It was obvious they wanted to see how she would handle a dancing, bobbing target on the water. Isla, let it land and move a foot downstream before blasting it out of the water.

The third try was only about three inches square. It hit the water and skimmed up and down and back up. It splintered on its last landing and in spite of the judge's warning, a round of applause broke out. The judge let it go.

The judge stood and looked at Isla who remained still, rifle down by her side. Neither surprise nor satisfaction on her face. There seemed to be little on the judge's face either. Maybe he was a poker player and was used to keeping his feelings hidden, or maybe what happened is what he was led to believe would happen. If there was relief or disappointment, nothing showed in his expression nor in his remarks.

"Thank you, Miss McNeese. Well done, I'm sure. Now as to the matter in front of us, the court finds no wrongdoing on the side of either party in this Buffalo Creek incident. You will not face charges for your part in injuring Mr. Bartram, the death of his horse nor the loss of his cattle. He will not face charges for trespassing on your property nor for the injury of the young man recuperating under your considerable hospitality. However, the sheriff will issue a warning to the both of you. I want this nonsense stopped and I want it stopped today. Any further progression of events will lead to arrests and incarcerations."

This time it was Deloris who broke out in applause. She couldn't help it, there was just too much joy. Her dad would not be arrested and her new best friend would not either, and there was a chance that life could change and she could be Alex's friend.

"We won't bother you anymore, ma'am. Please go back to life as you were and my congratulations again on your fine marksmanship. I've never seen the equal and that's no lie," the judge added.

"Your honor, there is a favor I would like to ask of the court."

"Please do, ma'am."

"I'm prepared to apply for my citizenship and I would like your honor to assist me with that."

"Splendid, the court would be more than happy to help in that worthy endeavor. When the spring thaw comes, bring your papers to my office and I and my staff will do all we can to make you a United States citizen."

The crowd dispersed to their horses, except for one of the extra witnesses. He took his horse's reins and moved up close to Isla. He removed his hat and slightly nodded. She had never seen him in Cheyenne, and she was sure he had never seen her. She waited.

"Miss McNeese, my name is Richard D. Wallace. I've recently moved to Cheyenne and like many others I have begun a new business. I would like a minute to talk to you about it if I may."

"Certainly, Mr. Wallace. I'm happy to meet you. Do you wish to come in or is outside all right for you?"

"It'll only take a minute and I don't want to be left too far behind the others. They might get suspicious. As I'm sure you've been told, winter is coming and when it gets here it will be almighty harsh. Perhaps harsher than anything you've known in your life. You are on a prairie and it's obvious that trees are scarce. At some point the buffalo chips will be gone or covered in snow. How will you cook and stay warm?

"That's where my new organization can help you. I'm bringing in hardwood from other sources and making it available to the settlers who are new here. I will deliver wood suitable for a cook stove to your yard and make sure you have it for the entire winter. How does that sound to you?"

"Depends on how much it cost and the terms of payment and the quality of the wood."

Mr. Wallace reached into his hip pocket and pulled out a folded sheet of paper. He unfolded it and handed it to Isla.

"Here is the cost, the promise, and the terms of payment. The sooner you can tell me your decision the better. There are a lot of newcomers, but I have a sense that you folks are going to survive somehow and I would like to be a part of it. This is going to be a great country before too much longer."

Isla read and reread the information. She looked Wallace in the eye. It was as important as the paper to her. She liked what was on the paper and she liked what was in his eyes.

"Please sign me up, Mr. Wallace. It can't be too soon as we are about to the end of our provisions of this type."

"Thank you. The first delivery will come to you next week and it will be unloaded and stacked at no extra charge. One other thing. The lumber yard still has a pile of odds and ends left over from cutting. I understand they will sell it reasonably cheap. Also, I noticed a pile of used railroad ties near the depot. Maybe your hand could go pick up a load before it's gone."

Isla's eyes brightened. "Thank you, Second John will start in the morning. This is wonderful news."

"Second John?"

"Yes, that's the hired man's name."

"Oh, I see."

"I doubt it, Mr. Wallace but it is what it is."

Part Two: Early Winter

But the valley did not tell me about winter,

How the flowers would die and hide their beauty in
the dirt.

It did not say the wind would chill the songs of birds
and man,

Or that the grasses would brown and weep,

Nor did it mention that the providers would move
south to warmer climes,

It did not mention the snow, the cold bitter snow that
hid the valley,

Nor did it recall that the nights were long and days
were too short for life.

There is no happiness in the valley in the winter,

But there is hope. There is always hope.

SEVENTEEN

The coming of winter was of course inevitable. It was preceded by a brief fall which was barely noticed among the inhabitants of Buffalo Creek. It came at first with enough time to make hurried preparations and thus the two homesteads worked around the clock, somehow sensing the necessity.

Second John went to Cheyenne for trip after trip, hauling mauled lumber, a few railroad ties, and various other things. His first stop in town was to see his friends at the general store. The owner warmly greeted him and then motioned him to a room behind the main counter.

"I thought you'd be in for some winter stuff. Been saving you something special." He motioned to a short stack of woolen blankets sitting on top of a nailed-up crate. "Saved a few of these for you. Going to be cold in that barn you're building."

Boards, blankets and a broken wood stove made it home on the first trip. Second John did not waste time splitting the wood up, but immediately returned for another load. He had spent winters in southeast Wyoming and knew what might be coming, especially out in an open area like Buffalo Creek.

He returned the next day to find Isla splitting the scrap lumber into small sticks suitable for the cooking stove. It was cold but she paused to wipe sweat from her forehead.

"Welcome home, Second John. Is the barn completely finished?"

"All but hanging a door. Got some likely-looking pieces on this load that I can use."

"I have a feeling you need to get it done. Every day seems colder even if it isn't."

"Yes ma'am. I'll finish it today. Soon as I unload this here pile of leftovers. You working too hard, Miss Isla."

"Good for me. I need to stay strong to take care of all you men."

"Yes, ma'am. How's young Alex?"

"Gaining strength. I shouldn't be surprised if he is out and about in a few days. The boy has a good attitude, you know, in spite of what happened."

"Ain't hurt none for young missus to visit him twice a week, I reckon."

"She reads to him and tells him stories from her childhood. Just to talk, you know. She's fallen for the boy, I'm afraid."

"What about him?"

"He doesn't talk about it to me. He's closed that way. But he's enjoying the attention, there's no doubt about that. He may be pretending to be hurting to keep Deloris coming. I believe in the power of love, Second John. What about you?"

"Let me think about that one, Miss Isla. I sure believe in the power of your love."

Isla smiled and to avoid spoiling the moment, took another practiced swing at a stout piece of lumber. The pile of cooking wood was growing and it brought a sense of satisfaction to her. There wasn't much they could do about the weather, but they were doing what they could to prepare.

Deloris' arrival was perfectly timed with the first freight wagon of hardwood. It was piled high and two large, strong-looking men road the box, the draft horses snorting at the slight incline.

"Where you want this firewood, miss?"

Isla stepped forward just past the new barn. "Between here and the creek but save room for a path by the creek. Is this all of it?"

"No, ma'am. We'll bring you one more load in two weeks. We're really busy and you shouldn't need any for a while anyway. Woah, Billy, woah, Bob. Set that brake hard, Charlie and let's get going. It's as far home as it was out here, I 'magine."

Isla wanted to go inside and supervise the reading visit, but she also wanted to take a good look at the wood she had purchased. She trusted Alex somewhat, but she wasn't sure about Deloris. The girl was growing bolder and bolder in her mind. Alex needed to be defended, even if he didn't know it.

I'm going to look silly running back and forth from the kitchen to the yard. How do I handle this?

She watched the unloading for a brief moment and satisfied with the firewood's quality, made her way into the house. She was surprised to find Alex sitting at the little table across from Deloris.

"Alex, are you okay?" Isla asked.

"Yes, ma'am. Tired of that bed and wanted a cup of your coffee. I got both. Deloris is reading a book she got from an aunt back east. It's about someone named Crane. Queer story, that's for sure."

"Do you think you could make it outside with some help from Deloris and me? There's lots of activity going on and not many non-freezing days left, I fear. Air would do you good. I'll take your left arm and Deloris your right. Come on, let's do it."

It was awkward but as things usually did when Isla got involved, the plan worked beautifully. Deloris and Alex admired the lumber Isla had split.

"That's a lot of firewood, Isla," Alex said.

"I'm afraid not, Alex," Deloris interrupted. "You haven't seen a Wyoming winter yet. That's a good start, but just a start. I predict several loads will be needed before the road closes."

All afternoon the temperature slowly fell dangerously toward the freezing mark. When the four of them were seated at the table enjoying their evening meal, Isla decided to broach what she saw as an oncoming problem.

"Gentlemen, I have a few words to say and I would like you to hear me out before interrupting and messing up my line of thought."

"I don't think we could do that, Isla," Frank said, "When you get on a topic, it's hard to move you off."

Isla was not in the mood. "I'm serious, Frank. This is important and we need to discuss it as a group, although I must admit my mind is mostly made up."

"We're listening," Alex said and cast a glare at his brother.

"From all reports we heard from town, from Deloris, the Gardeners, and from the signs Second John has shared, it appears we are in for a bitter cold spell in the very near future. Three of us have no experience with that kind of cold, according to Second John, and need to take his advice. Which leads me to say you should heed my advice after hearing his.

"We have three buildings and four people, one of whom is still recovering. The buildings are small and so are the spaces. None of them are adequately heated, nor can they be. Our only hope of survival, I feel sure, is that we share the resources we have.

"Therefore, I suggest the Jamisons close their building up and move what they can over here to this side of the creek. There's room in the barn, in the horse stable, for Alex and Frank to put their beds. Second John's stove will help a little. Second John has blankets as well.

"We will combine our food efforts and the work efforts to one site till the worst is over. We will share the discomfort, but we will also share the overcoming of the storm, such as it be. Any questions?"

Alex looked at Frank and Frank looked at Second John. "What do you say, Second John?"

"Miss Isla's right. No other way. You're doomed in that place of yours and not much better here."

"Okay, Alex and I are in but we have to be able to pull our weight. Tomorrow I'm taking Maude and the wagon and heading north for aways. We will need more meat than we have now. I'll try to find some deer, elk or antelope for drying."

"Don't go too far, Frank. We don't know when this bad weather is coming."

"Don't worry about me, Isla, I'm a grown man and can take care of myself. I survived a war, I can survive a deer hunt, I think."

"I want to go with you, Frank. I can drive the wagon and help set up camp. I'm not much good here," Alex said.

"No, Alex," Isla said, "you're going to help keep a fire in the kitchen and feed the chickens and milk the cow. You aren't completely healed, you know. A ride on that buckboard would set you back. That will leave me free to help with the heavier work."

Second John also had a plan, "I'll need to borrow a horse because I need to go to town and pick up several coils of rope. If a blizzard hits we'll be blinded and stuck in whatever building we happen to be in. I'll rope paths to connect all the buildings together so we won't get lost."

"What about the livestock, Second John," Isla asked.

"Up to them and God, I guess. No telling where they'll wind up. We'll deal with that later."

The next morning dawned cold and clear. As soon as a hearty breakfast was shared, the hunting party and the rope party left to take care of their tasks. Isla gave Alex instructions on her stove, the wood, the chickens and the proper way to care for the milk. She then went to splitting lumber and wood.

The sky became milky as gray clouds began to drift in. There was a slight shift in the wind, bringing it in from the southwest and the nearest mountains. It was not a good sign. There was no visit from Deloris and there would be none for the next several weeks. However, a visitor did show up in the middle of the morning.

Carla, dressed in a warm sheepskin coat and heavy wool scarf, rode into the newly formed wood yard. Isla laid down her ax, happy for an excuse to relax tired muscles.

"Hello, Carla. Won't you light down and come in? I've got a pot boiling and it's a lot warmer in the house."

"No thank you, Isla. I'll be quick, as this weather is set on the edge of changing and not for the better. I want you to know that Ryan and I are concerned about you newcomers to the valley and we want to try to help in some way. The four of you will need a lot of food to make it through and we don't think you have it. Ryan is sending some hands over after lunch with a few steers and a dozen hens. Hopefully, it will help. If worse comes to worst we want the four of you to come to the ranch at the first break in the weather. No arguments, this is serious business."

Isla watched Carla's retreating back. How fortunate they had made such friends as the Gardeners. The beef would be welcomed and so would the extra eggs, if they could keep the hens alive. She felt better in spite of the negative warnings, but the feeling was short-lived.

The rhythmic sound of the ax was broken by the bellowing of thirsty and angry cattle. Isla looked up and her heart fell faint. Coming to the water directly across from her outbuildings was a large herd of steers pushed along by Rocking AB cowboys. There was no Jake Meadows and no August Bartram, but they were Bartram's cattle nevertheless, and they were back on her land. Hundreds of them.

No need to guess as to Bartram's frame of mind, or if he had mellowed any. Here was the evidence that he still intended to impose his will and at the worst possible time. The steers muddied the water and churned up the bank. Then they began what they came to do and that was to drink from the creek and devour the last of the thick prairie grass along the creek.

Isla knew she was defeated. She was by herself and could not possibly move that many animals alone. She and the men would have to move way upstream to find unpolluted water and the smell from the cattle would become noxious. Just as she was ready to forgive Bartram, he found a way to raise her ire.

I will not let it change me. I will not let it change the Jamisons. I will not let it defeat us. There will be no surrender nor pleading for mercy. You want me to escalate, Bartram, but I won't. I will let God judge between you and me. God will provide. He has and he will. God have mercy on your soul, August Bartram. You are not worthy of the ground you cherish nor the water you desire.

The hunter returned two days later, both pleased and angry. He had killed two elk and managed to cut them up and haul them back. There was plenty of wood to smoke the large animals and the process began immediately. The sight of the cattle scattered along the bank nearly made him lose control. He was headed for his horse, grim and purposeful. It was time to put an end to this offensive human. He never made it to his horse. Second John grabbed his arm and held him back.

"No need, Frank. Bartram has outsmarted himself. He's provided us with all the food we need for the winter, free of charge. I'll help you with the elk."

Frank stopped and looked at the milling steers. A slow grin spread across his beaded face. "That's a good one, Second John. I'll be sure to tell him thank you later on."

EIGHTEEN

Isla and Frank sat across the table from each other, sipping coffee and enjoying the slight warmth of the room. Alex occasionally fed wood scraps to the cooking stove. The remains of supper sat on the top of the iron surface in case someone wanted another biscuit or piece of beef steak. The door opened and Second John turned sideways, maneuvering a load of stove-cut hardwood. He stacked it next to the dwindling building scraps.

"It's coming," he said in his economy of words. "I feel it. It's coming and it's coming hard. Wear your clothes to bed and wrap up with everything else."

"Would you like some coffee and maybe a biscuit, Second John," Isla asked.

"That'd be good. Everyone needs to eat all they can to warm the insides."

Alex opened the fire door and poked a stick in the burner. "How long will the stove burn without more wood?"

"If you get it real hot like for baking, it'll last up to three hours. For one thing, ashes need to be removed regularly," Isla said. "it's a good stove but not large and certainly not built to heat a house in this kind of cold."

"Wear a scarf over your ears even in bed; extra socks, too." Second John added.

"I'm wondering," Alex said, "if it's going to be as cold as Second John thinks if we should all stay in here and one of us take turns keeping the fire going. Couldn't we do that?"

"We can have you men bring your bed things and all the blankets and make pallets on the floor. One of us up getting wood and the others sleeping. It would be rough, I guess, but we could do it. I'm for trying," Isla said.

Second John, paused on his second biscuit for a moment, "We can at least keep from freezing. We may be too cold to sleep."

"The three of us will do it, Isla. You're not going out in any storm for wood. The three of us can handle a third of the night. I wish we had some playing cards or dominoes or something," Frank said.

"I'll take my turn, Frank."

"No, you take care of the cooking and we'll do the rest of the work. Right men? We need you to stay healthy and going in and out may not be so healthy."

"What about the poor Indians, like the ones who stopped by here?" Alex asked.

"Generations of exposure have conditioned them. Their teepees keep off the sun, not the cold. They cover their skin with thick bear grease and sleep together under heavy buffalo robes," Second John said.

Frank drew the first watch and all of the men went for their bed rolls and extra blankets and wraps. Goodnights were said and the lamp turned down low. It was decided to keep it near the stove so that the person feeding the fire would avoid accidents. Frank had a dog-eared copy of New England Verse and he was soon immersed in its contents. No one had a timepiece, so it was decided that he would stay awake as long as he could and then wake Alex up. They would make it through the first night with confidence.

The storm did not come on sly foxes' feet but on the onrushing paws of running coyotes. It came hard and fast and ugly and mostly, relentless. It began at midnight and grew in rage, destroying any concept of morning or daylight. It came with wind and bitter cold and then dry snow. Lots of snow, blowing sideways and piling over everything, landing in low places like the front door. It piled on the downwind side of the roof, and it pushed against the sod.

The cattle tried to turn and move before it. They stumbled and cried out, the snow converging in their ears, eyes and noses. Roy gave up his charges and huddled between the barn and the chicken house. The snow-covered him over and, in the process, saved his life.

Alex was gathering a load of wood from the hardwood stacks when it hit. The suddenness of it took him aback and he lost his footing and dropped the load of wood nestled in his arms. The onslaught of snow stung his face and exposed his hands and temporarily blinded him. Nothing Second John, Deloris, or the Gardeners had said prepared him for the reality of the roaring storm.

He bent down, using the woodpile as a shield and picked the fallen pieces up. Once on his feet, the wind took him towards the house. Even then, he was wondering how he could come back for another load. He looked at the rope leading to the front door. *If he held the rope, he could only carry wood in one hand.* He shook his head, not in defeat but in defiance. *They would figure out something.*

Once back inside, he realized how cold his fingers were. In those few minutes he was exposed, they were already tingling. He touched his nose. Nothing. He added wood and pulled a chair up closer to the stove itself. In the short moment of opening and closing the outside door the temperature in the room had dropped. The wind changed decibels, alternating between a painful groaning and a high-pitched scream. He found his gloves and put them on to warm his hands. He also retrieved a scarf from his coat pocket and wrapped it around his ears.

He looked at his sleeping companions and he wanted to wake them. He was afraid. He put another split piece of wood in the chamber. The stove was hot now but the room was not. He walked to Isla's door and listened in. She was not snoring but she was asleep. He thought he should open the bedroom door. The heat was not penetrating through the rough barrier and it was noticeably colder away from the stove.

He eased the door open a little and the cold that hit him in the face sent chills down his back to his feet. The fear hit him again. He stared at his friend, buried under various covers and one of Second John's blankets. Maybe she was warm, he said to himself. But, not outside those covers; not the cold air she was breathing in. A shiver hit him and he quickly backed up to his chair by the stove. He counted the remaining firewood. Enough for an hour or two at most.

The storm and the night advanced. Visibility outside became near zero. No moon or stars in the Wyoming sky could withstand the ferocity of the wind and snow. The snow blew horizontally, swirling and twisting around and over every obstacle. Silently the creek crept under a thin coating of ice and snow, keeping the brook trout warm enough to survive. The wood froze and cracked under the pressure of the sinking temperature. Hands and fingers struggled with it, but the wood caravan continued through the night. Gloves, scarves and hats tied on with scarves offered little protection.

On Second John's last trip before the night ended, he returned to the house with a small bundle that looked nothing like firewood. He sat the snow-covered Roy on the floor near the stove and began to rub the dog's wiry fur. Roy made no sound other than very shallow breathing. The burial in the snow had kept him from freezing but the cold was overcoming him.

The snow melted off his fur and formed a puddle. Second John moved Roy to a dry spot and started rubbing again. Then he picked the little dog up and placed him under his coat, pulling the covering close against him. Isla found the two of them asleep in front of the stove when she rose to begin breakfast.

Once the biscuit dough was rising, Isla began cutting whole potatoes up, skin and all, into the largest pot she owned. The butter from the previous day also went into the pot and the remainder of the milk. Next, she took a large slice of smoked brisket and began cutting it into thin slices, which she planned on frying along with the large bowl of eggs waiting to be cracked.

In spite of the cold, the spreading aroma reached into the nooks and crannies of the little house and sleeping men began wrinkling their noses and coming to life. All except Second John. He had been up a long time and his search for Roy had left him spent. Isla carefully stepped around him to get the cups out and pour the first cup of coffee. She looked at the awaking men. She didn't know how because she had been asleep, but somehow, their worst fears had not overtaken them and they were all still alive and well.

Frank sent Alex out to feed the chickens and milk Maggie while he made the first of the morning woodpile trips.

"Where's the sun, Frank," Isla asked.

"No sun, Isla. There was no moon or stars and there is no sun. Just wind and snow and cold. We must do today what we did last night. We will survive and we will be strong because with the good Lord's help, we won. I'm thinking a Bible reading of thanksgiving would be appropriate before we eat. Speaking of eating, the smell of that food is calling my name."

Alex popped in the door, stepped round Second John and placed the container of milk on the small shelf next to the stove. "Maggie's not happy and she doesn't look good. It's so cold out there I don't know how she survived the night."

"Did you see the cattle or horses, Alex?" Isla asked.

"You can't see anything, Isla. Barely your fingers in front of your face. Can't hear anything but wind and blowing snow, either. The cattle could be ten feet away or ten thousand and I wouldn't know the difference. Doesn't matter. We can't do a thing about a thing, I'm thinking."

Isla shook Second John and divested him of Roy. "Come on, Second John, eat and then get in bed. It's going to be a long day from Alex's report."

In and out the wood bearers went and lunch and then supper came and passed. The second night started much as the first except they knew more of what to do and expect. The cold did not abate nor did the wind-driven snow. Ashes went outside and fresh wood came in. People talked or slept. Frank shared his book of poetry and the group discussed the poems from England.

The second morning, Isla left her bed and bundled up as tight as she could, she made her way to the barn. She wanted to see Maggie for herself; the sight nearly broke her down. She found an extra ration of corn and spread it in the manger. She was worried because Maggie struggled to give the normal amount of milk.

"You're our only source of milk, cream and butter, Maggie. You can't dry up now. Not in the middle of winter. You have to make it to spring. I can't take you in the house and the corn and two bags of grain is all there is. Hang on, girl. This will pass. I'm sure it will pass."

Two days later Isla woke up coughing, her head burning with fever and her usual strength sapped. Frank stepped into her room and stood by her bedside. He reached down and touched her forehead. Isla struggled to rise.

"No, ma'am. You are not leaving that bed. You're sick. You went outside two days ago, right?"

She nodded weakly and tried to speak, but coughing came instead. Frank went for a wet cloth. When he returned, Isla was shaking as chills ran down her body.

"Alex," Frank called. "Bring one of the blankets in here and hurry. Isla is bad sick."

The three men took turns sitting next to their lady friend but it was Frank who was there the majority of the time. The others tried to pry him away, but he refused. He left to go outside for wood and to the other room to eat. He wiped her head to cool her fever and held her hand to calm her spirits and read poems and psalms into the night. Even when she would lapse into sleep, he would continue to read or talk.

He told her everything about himself and how he felt about her. Things he had not known before to tell. Seeing her in pain and agony pressed him into the hands of God as never before. He tried to tell her how she had changed his life, but the words didn't seem adequate enough. Second John and Alex took on all the work. Second John cooked what he could and then, as suddenly as it came, the storm went.

It did not pause to say goodbye or even I'm sorry. Sometime during the sixth night it moved out, leaving snow and dead animals scattered across the prairie. No one cheered its passing, just as no one missed its presence. Every day it warmed a degree or two. No quick thaw or sudden change, just overall improvement.

Frank looked down at Isla. Her face now pink instead of red. Her breath labored but not strained with coughing. She had no energy but she needed none as all she had to do was look up at Frank.

"I love you," he said.

"I know," she answered.

"I mean, I love you with all my heart and soul."

"I wouldn't want it any other way. I feel the same about you."

"Can I kiss you?"

"You might get sick."

"No, I won't get sick. I've been right here day and night."

Her eyes held a moment of clarity, "I'll take a chance then."

He touched his lips to hers gently. Aware of men in the other room. She reached for his head and pulled him closer.

"Alex..." he started to say.

"Close the door, Frank."

NINETEEN

The first one up on the next day following the storm was Isla. It was the first time she beat the men to the stove since becoming sick. She was humming, a sure sign that she felt better. The stove fire had gone out so someone had failed to do their job before turning in. There were a few hot coals in the grey ashes and she was able to get a small fire started with some kindling. She slid the coffee pot across the stove to the large front burner and the slight noise brought Second John upright on his pallet. He quickly threw his blankets aside and got to his feet.

"Miss Isla, what are you doing? Sit down, please."

"Second John, if you want coffee and breakfast, you better get me some firewood and I don't mean sooner or later."

Second John pulled on his boots, grabbed his old coat with the sheepskin lining and bolted out the door. The coffee pot was followed by an iron skillet which went on the other front burner. Isla sliced the shoulder of pork and put the thin strips in the pan. The stove was just hot enough for the bacon to send tendrils of aroma into the tight room. First one and then the other Jamison brother sat up on their pallets rubbing their eyes. No man worth his salt could sleep through the smell of boiling coffee and frying bacon.

Alex was on his feet first. "Good morning, Isla. Why are you cooking?"

"Why shouldn't I be cooking?"

"You've been sick."

"Yes, but this morning I'm better, and it's time I got my job back. Now you do yours and get us some eggs and fresh milk."

"I'll get the milk but I don't think there'll be any eggs."

"Why not?"

"While you were so sick, the chickens all died. At least, we think they did. No one's seen any and it's been bitter cold."

"I guess the chickens are frozen so we can thaw them and cook them later. No eggs. Well, at least we'll have milk and I can make biscuits. We still have flour if no eggs. Hurry, milk Maggie and I'll see what else I can scrape up."

Alex closed the door behind him and Frank materialized next to Isla. He put his arms around her and pulled her close. "Are you sure you are well enough to be up? Here, you sit down and I'll take over."

"I'm fine, Frank. You check those bags along the wall and see if there are some grits or potatoes hiding out. With no eggs, we need a little more to eat. I'll start some biscuit dough."

The door opened and Second John entered with a load of split stove wood and a blast of cold air. He lay the wood in the wood box and started feeding the stove.

"It's gone," he said to the room.

"What's gone?" Isla and Frank asked like an echo in a canyon.

"The storm. It's gone. Cold is still here but the wind is gone. Sun coming."

Frank grabbed the door and opened it. Isla moved beside him. The sun was just visible but the pink and orange rays spreading across the horizon were evidence of clearer skies and heavenly light.

"Shut the door, Frank, you're freezing me," Isla laughed. "Have you ever seen anything as beautiful?"

Second John finished feeding the stove and Frank went in search of potatoes or grits. The door opened again to admit Alex. He sat the milk pail down on the table.

"Hope nobody had their heart set on a big glass of milk. I only got half a pail. I don't think Maggie has had enough water. It freezes faster than you can bust it up. The creek is harder than ever. We may need the pickaxe to get through."

"I'll tackle it after breakfast," Second John said, "without the wind, it'll seem like summer."

"Gosh, I can tell the difference inside, already. I can feel the heat from the stove way over here. Maybe if the sun does get up it'll warm the outside up. Hey, I think we can eat breakfast without our coats on," Alex said.

Frank raised up from the far wall, a medium burlap bag in his hand. "Look at what I found. An unopened bag of course-ground grits."

"Bring them here quick. I'll wash some and get them to boiling. Grits, bacon, biscuits and coffee may not be fit for a king, but it'll sure do common folks. We won't think about the eggs...or the chickens," Isla said.

When the last bite was sopped up with the last biscuit, Second John excused himself and eased out the door. Frank and Alex looked at each other.

"You want the chickens or the woodpile?" Frank asked.

"I'll take care of the chickens and see after Maggie," Alex answered.

"I'll help with the chickens," Isla said.

"Please, Isla, stay inside one more day. Maybe tomorrow will be warmer. You're better, but you're not out of the woods completely. Catch up on some things in here and let us handle the outside."

She looked at Frank. He was so pitiful in his concern for her. "All right. I'll stay in one more day but that's all. I need to see the sun just like the rest of you do."

TWENTY

They were finishing the second baked chicken when they heard it. Isla shushed the conversation. "What's that sound?"

Everyone tuned in to the faint murmur. They knew what it was, but it was so unexpected that it took a minute for it to register.

"It's water dripping," Second John said.

"It's not warm enough to melt the snow," Alex said.

"No, but the stove pipe is. Without the wind factor, the warmth of the pipe is melting the snow around the pipe itself," Frank said, "it's not above freezing but the sun is warming the air just a mite."

"It'll turn back cold tonight, won't it, Second John?" Isla asked.

Second John nodded, "Yes, but not as cold as last night and the sun will be warm again tomorrow."

"We've made it," Frank said. "We've survived. Thank you, God."

For three straight days, the sun grew warmer and the wind hid behind the mountains. On the third day melting snow began to trickle from the roof of the cabin on Buffalo Creek. The ice on the creek thinned and patches of clear water appeared. Isla was tired of beef and chickens. She wanted to try for trout and so she found a place that was clear of ice and using small scraps of meat, she added brook trout to the sack until she had enough for a full meal for everyone.

Maggie and Roy moved to the creek. Roy ran up and down for most of the day looking for his cows but had no luck.

Maggie drank deep from the creek bank and pulled on some of the dead grass that was now free of snow.

On the fourth day, the unexpected happened. Just before lunch, Balloch walked up the trace to the house. He came from the south, but no one knew from how far. Later in the afternoon, he was joined by Frank's and Alex's horses. Their coats were thick and wooly, but they looked thin and uncared for. That was soon remedied with grain and brushes.

"Think we could find those cows?" Frank asked Second John.

"Could be. They drifted with the horses, is my guess."

Frank brought the idea up at supper. "Second John and I think we'll go look for the cattle in the morning. If the weather holds, I thought Alex might take the wagon to town and get some groceries and grain. What do you think?"

"I think they're my cows."

"No one is debating whose cows they are, Isla. We're just trying to divide up the labor. You want to go look for cows with Second John, I'll stay here and take care of the chores around the homestead."

"Whoa. I didn't mean to upset you. Makes sense for me to stay and you to go. I'm not sure I'm up to a hard ride. You two go. I've more than enough to do here."

"You sure?"

"I'm sure, Frank. I'm still not used to being looked after by a man who cares."

"I'm ready to make it permanent."

"I know. I know. I'm thinking."

After breakfast, Alex harnessed Maude to the buckboard and headed towards Cheyenne to replenish their supplies. He pulled his heavy coat around his shoulders and secured a blanket over his knees and feet. Maude was well rested and set off at a good pace. Alex held the reins in both hands and talked to Maude for a few miles and then began talking to himself.

I'm so lucky to be alive and able to drive a wagon all the way to Cheyenne. I wonder about Bartram. He's probably up and about as well. That means as soon as they round up their cattle, he'll send them back to Isla's. She should have shot him and not the horse. I wonder what the Judge would do if he knew that Bartram had disobeyed the court's order? Maybe he would send the sheriff to arrest him. If he went to jail, that would give us a chance to get started good without him messing with us and Isla. I've got to hurry but I think I'll take time to visit the sheriff.

What about Deloris, though? You're sweet on her, aren't you, Alex? She cares about you too but the business with her dad is in the way. If I turn him in, she'll hate me. Maybe they won't tell her who told

Second John caught up Roy and held him across his lap as he rode onto the trace. No one knew how far it would be before they encountered the missing cows and Second John figured Roy might as well be rested. Maybe the cows would want to come home, or maybe they wouldn't. He and Frank rode at a steady trot down the south side of the creek for three hours and then they came upon a large group of cattle crowded around a wide place in the creek. There was a mixture of cows, steers and a few bulls.

"Do you know which ones are Isla's?" Second John asked.

"No, I don't. If they aren't branded or marked, we'll separate them out. Leave the steers and bulls and marked cows. If some aren't hers, their owners can come and claim them later."

The two men turned wranglers and with a lot of help from Roy, soon had a fairly good-sized herd rounded up. As far as Frank could tell, they all looked like cows to him and he wasn't sure anyone could say, "That dark brown cow is mine or that spotted one with the broken horn belongs to me."

They were soon on their way back to Isla's homestead with twice the number of cows she had lost. They had to pull the brim of their hats down due to the glare of the sun reflecting off the snow. It felt good, but they also sensed the cold that was in the air. A small breeze picked up and they urged the cows to move a little faster. It would be better to get to the small ranch before the sun actually set.

Roy was kept busy as the larger herd of cows was not disposed to move back to the west. They were enjoying their freedom and some were unfamiliar with feisty cattle dogs.

The balmy weather lasted two more days. It turned out that two days was enough. Isla was thinking of going to the Gardeners to see if they could spare two or three layers when a call came from down the trace.

"Hello, the house," rang unexpectedly through the morning air. The loud and unfamiliar voice startled everyone.

The small community of friends had been working hard and fast, knowing the time was short before the next blast of cold wind and snow came upon them. Two loads of firewood had been stacked near the door and sacks of grain and food supplies had been stored inside the house. There wasn't much they could do about the livestock.

Isla opened the door to see three riders coming up the trace towards her door. Two were strangers, but one was not. She recognized the middle rider as August Bartram. Something was odd about the scene and it took her a moment to realize what it was. Rancher Bartram's wrists were bound together and he was holding the saddle horn in his fists rather than the reins.

The other two men were wearing silver stars on the front of their leather vests. She saw them as their mackinaws moved from side to side. August Bartram had obviously been arrested, but for some reason, it gave her no joy. Perhaps in view of the struggles of the past several weeks, it seemed anticlimactic.

The lead rider tipped his hat and spoke to her. "Miss McNeese? I'm Chad Pennington, U.S. Marshal for the Wyoming Territory. My deputy here is Benjamin McCabe. I believe you know Mr. Bartram."

Isla looked at the deputy and saw for the first time that he was a black man. She had not seen a black person since leaving Denver. He also touched the brim of his hat and smiled at her. His teeth were very white and his smile was contagious. She smiled back.

"How can I help you gentlemen?" she asked the marshal but did not take her eyes off August Bartram. He stared back and she could feel the hatred from fifteen feet away. *I'm sorry for you, Bartram, but you were warned. I'm glad to see you up and on a horse, though. You look pale and weak and strangely defiant. I will pray for you while you are in prison that God will soften your heart.*

"The judge asked us to stop by and tell you that Mr. Bartram was in custody for defying a court order. He seemed to think it would be important to you. Is it?"

"Yes, and no. Yes, if his hired hands stay off my land."

"I think Ben and I persuaded them to leave you and your homestead alone, but if they don't, just send for us. We'll close the ranch down if we have to. Mr. Bartram may not be back for a while."

Bartram uttered an oath and then addressed the marshals though he was looking at Isla, "That woman tried to kill me and I'm the one being arrested? That's not justice. But I will have justice, judge or no judge, marshal or not! I'll be back, McNeese, so you better pick a burial plot. On second thought, the prairie will do just fine for your Scottish carcass."

Isla was shocked at the sight of the gap in Bartram's front teeth. There was a slight whistling sound as he spoke, which made it hard to understand some words. She did not mention it as she knew it would only make matters worse.

"Your neighbors will pray for your heart that it might soften and we will take care of your daughter until it does.

"What about Deloris?" Isla asked, ignoring Bartram's threat.

"Is that Miss Bartram, the daughter?" Marshal Pennington asked, hoping to end the rant coming from his prisoner.

"Yes."

"We left her in tears. I would say she is a mixed-up person at the moment. She understood why her father was arrested, but it didn't make her any happier. I'm assuming she is alone there on the ranch."

"Yes, she is. The head wrangler will look after her. One of us will go see about her as soon as we can. I think we might be in for another blow by tonight, though."

"Yes, ma'am. Cold snap tonight, maybe some snow. If you'll excuse us, we'll see if we can't get to Cheyenne before it hits. I have a pregnant wife and I don't want her to be alone."

Bartram interrupted the marshal, "You better leave my daughter..."

"Shut up, Bartram! Else my deputy will shut you up and it will hurt!"

"Thank you, marshal, and thank you for stopping and telling us what happened and a safe journey home to you.

"Will Mr. Bartram go to jail?" Isla added.

"I think that's the idea, Miss McNeese. He's made a good judge angry and that's never a wise thing. I don't think these latest threats to you will wear well with the judge, either. Good day, folks."

The marshals and their prisoner turned and hurried down the trace to the stagecoach road. Isla heard scuffling and looked behind her. The three men had all left their jobs and came down to see what was going on. Alex had the biggest grin on his face.

"Isla, I'd give anything to have one of them cameras I heard about. I'd sure put a picture of old man Bartram tied up between marshals on my wall."

"What do we do about Deloris?" she asked.

"I'll go check on her. She helped me," Alex said.

In a moment, he fled down the trace riding bareback as if his life depended on it. Isla looked at Frank and Second John.

She smiled, "The bad man is gone, but the work is still here for those who aren't intent on rescue. What do you say? Storm tonight, are we ready for number two?"

How long will Alex stay at the Rocking AB? Frank wondered as he took Isla by the arm and escorted her to the small home on Buffalo Creek.

Part Three: Spring

Spring came to the valley, not so much reluctantly as
cautious.

I was waiting for it, so it was not a surprise.

The snow melted and the wind, ever blowing,
warmed.

The sky blued to a perfect hue and the sun called the
flowers up,

The long-stemmed grasses reached for the heavens
and waved.

Newly hatched insects rose into the circulating air,

And the trout joined them in celebration,

Everywhere, new life joined in the celebration.

Frank asked me again, and I said, "YES."

The End

Other Westerns by Philip Dampier

The Creek: A Western Love Story

The Spring

Dakota Marshal

The Sorrel Mare

Romance

A Faded Rose

The Robert H. and Tisza Series

The Red Shoe (1)

The Old Man on the Mountain (2)

The Third Witness (3)

Collateral Damage (4)

Can't Lose Her (5)

Chasing Money (6)

The Robin Hood Project (7)

The Raker (8)

Other Books by Philip Dampier

Can't Catch Me

Hitchhiking USA

The Five Wise Men

The Last Hunt and Other Stories

Comments on Verses from the Psalms (non-fiction)

Comments on Galatians (non-fiction)

To the Faithful Saints at Ephesus (non-fiction)